NEW PLAINS PRESS
AUBURN, ALABAMA

LEECHDOM

LEECHDOM

A Novel • Lee Tyler Williams

Library of Congress Control Number: 2015953319
ISBN: 9780985770389

Lee Tyler Williams, 1983 -
Leechdom

Published by Summerfield Publishing
New Plains Press
PO Box 1946
Auburn, AL, 36831-1946
newplainspress.com

The text of this book is composed in Centaur.

This is a work of fiction, and any resemblances between the stories, settings, and characters to any real people, places, or events is, well, fiction.

Behold thou ruthless feast
   As hosts burn their altars
   And thou supplicant kneels
   Before the pyres to pose
   The riddle of awakening

   ~The Canticle of St. Ursula

The Lord is not limitless, but the distance required for the soul to reach Him is. Though the circle possesses no center, wherever you stand is the furthest distance possible from any vestige of grace. For some of the faithful, suffering readies the soul for redemption and yet for others it calcifies the soul so it may plunge to unremembered depths. How can suffering render two souls as thus without possessing in itself some attributes that surpass all knowing? Many sisters attest to divine prescience of its domain, as if by tending to it they somehow imbibe it as their own. Yet suffering itself is not the essence of a soul in ascent. To suffer, one must cling to the earthly self: it sets before us a ledger of tasks that achieve, if carried out dutifully, the abandonment of flesh.

The patients suffered because of their past enjoining with the world of man. Some in the camp morosely accepted their banishment, fashioning themselves as students of the forest's decay and rejuvenation. The languid onslaught of the tide. The ceaseless melting of wood and fruit and earth. The dirt festering beneath the loose cabin floorboards bore this acrid ageless fluid. Others held the idiocy of man to blame for their banishment and railed against any apostle of the unafflicted world. Precisely because they so loathed the world, many of them did not wish to escape the camp.

I was washing the Mother's foul sweat from her linens when an empty raft floated past. Canerows on the other side of the river were scattered by the wind and seeped into dusk. Beneath the levee, mosquitoes clouded around my legs and spread the same poison that was killing the Mother. Shortly after her fever broke, I had caught her further up the bend, kneehigh in water, wearing her underskirt and no cornice while the bell was ringing downriver. She had hung her beads from the branch of a lone chinaberry. All that morning she had been in her bedchamber, screaming that the house was a great beast. After drifting further out, she pleaded for me to pull her ashore and when I stepped into the water she plunged beneath and thrashed against the current. She thought I was her Mother and said she didn't want to go to the city.

I took what linen dried overnight and left it folded at the top of the stairs. The door to her bedchamber was closed. In my room, I lifted my underskirt and ran my fingers over my legs, but no poison had swollen beneath them. The patients had been in the yard all day restlessly awaiting the Mother to deliver meals, prepare gauze, and lead catechism, but she was locked in her room and her breathing rattled through the house.

Sister M. called us to the Mother's bedchamber, and Sister E. and I sat beside her bed, entranced by her convulsions. The windows were draped, and the breath of our prayers caused the candleflames to shudder. Sister M. held her hand whispering, We hang our harps upon the willows in the midst thereof. The Mother's bared eyes reminded me of the near blind boy's when he lifted them to the sun.

For they that carried us away captive required of us a song. Sing us one of the songs of Zion. How shall we sing the Lord's song in a strange land, the Mother asked. Sister M. daubed her brow and quieted her by putting her finger to her lips.

In my vision of the frozen tide, ice snapped in ornate lines that widened as the riverbanks further divided. Each ripple was sustained perfectly so that some edges of the water were bladelike while the shoals rendered dull encircling ridges. The wind lifted shavings of ice into kneehigh vortices that churn outward, coating the cypress grove.

I idled from the bend back to camp as water melted over the reeds and mud seeped into the grass, reached my boots, and crawled up my legs. Washing had been tossed from the line, and egrets perched in rows on the roof lifted their wings.

When I awoke I saw smoke lifting from the wick. I dressed quickly in the mirror shard and repeated two questions breathlessly as if they comprised a prayer. How may evil instruct us to renounce the world? Or how can we not fail to renounce the world in missteps for evil rarely appears continuously and will fade from the memory of the wicked and appear in the face of the meek?

Downstairs I heard flies and walked to the dining room and saw them circling the tablecloth. By the time I delivered breakfast the wind was burning with the smell of rain. It was hot enough that the men had pinned canvas across the windowholes of their cabin. As I passed out bowls to them, I asked for the whereabouts of Paul. Another patient, Charles, said he had lost in blackjack and escaped. The sergeant muttered he hoped the sonofabitch drowned.

The day before I had seen Paul from the kitchen stoop walking along the house and peering under the crawlspace with a knife at his side. He said he was hunting for muskrat and did not excuse himself for being in the yard at that hour. Before I asked him to return to his cabin, he had shuffled along the house, lisping with his ravaged tongue for the creatures to come out.

I conferred with no one regarding my vision of the frozen tide. The warm air and the reeds thawing. Shoals opened upon glistening passages where no vessel sounded. The river, a pathway that all creatures of land fear to cross. A crane may alight before fluttering to ascend. Fish eternally afloat with their bloodshot eyes. Eucalypti bend toward the mist. Sparrow song remained stale and impatient while ospreys prowled on their music, and mist captured each bog lily in its purest hue as they drifted like greek fire along with the incoming thunderheads.

Many sisters of the apostolic orders fear the possibilities intrinsic to an unfolding landscape such as the one I envisioned. Their vows predicate engagement with the outer reaches of the godly, and yet they prefer musty chambers and corridors. Labyrinths to charm their isolation.

A boy arrived from town with a letter issued in reply to our request for a priest. The letter had arrived nearly a month after the post date. It bore no stamp. Both the envelope and page somewhat resembled vellum in scent and texture. The Church had received our request. Further summoning would occur in due course. Unsigned. I resealed the envelope and set it on the parlor desk where Sister M. had lately been shuffling through the accounts, assuming more of the Mother's daily tasks while she spoiled her tabby with fishbone.

I could see terror in Sister M.'s face when she came downstairs and informed us of the Mother's death. She allowed each of us to make our final round of the bedchamber. Inside, the shutters were lifted and curtains pulled back, igniting dust into a frantic churning. The room seemed no less responsible for her death than the poison in her veins.

I stared at her and held her hand, wanting to ask her if an angel were wronged, would it not seek revenge by plaguing our camp with a curse? And yet which sin could compel an angel to revenge? Which virtue could dissuade an angel from delivering mayhem? I finally let go of her hand when I heard the other two conversing beyond the door and rushed down the hallway to my bedchamber. In the first year of the camp, workers under the sheriff's command constructed a chapel behind the house. It resembled almost identically the barn closer to the woodline. However, the chapel had two doors with carvings that formed a cross when latched together and the roof was capped with a cross. Sister M. said that without a priest the Mother's resting would be farcical, and we abstained from the dousing of holy water. After we enveloped her body in linens and wrapped it in burlap shreds, its dampness stained the fabric.

We carried her across the walkway slats and into the chapel and laid her in the center of the floor. The dust pressed from beneath her in a cloud that pulled at the candleflames lining the altar. Her head was placed towards the altar in acknowledgement of her stature in the years since the priest's abandonment. She would read verses to the patients who huddled on the benches or lingered in their wheelchairs against the walls, and she had absolved two of them by graveside. They likewise addressed her as Mother and spoke of her often as their own progenitor, notwithstanding her bouts of wrath in which she reminded them that their souls were among the unborn and the undead and the sins of their fathers had fouled their limbs and the Lord had yet to forgive them.

That night the emptiness of the house awoke and slowly filled each room, arriving with wind through the servant's passage until it spilled through the door bowed by rot into the upstairs hallway. I dreamt of a body drifting downriver, facedown with limbs outstretched. An army of bullheads latched to its face. The clothes had been shredded, and its back protruded with pustules yellowed in the glare of the sun. A raft floated by. The man standing atop it pulled the body onboard. As the raft slid into the reeds, I saw that the face of the man resembled Paul, the butcher whose customers gossiped about the rash around his mouth and his broken tongue until a crowd gathered outside his abattoir threatening to burn him out unless he surrendered. Before his likely lynching, the police intervened and sent him to the holding terminal, or what the patients called the pesthole.

When God punished those who sinned in the land of Judaea, he infected them with pale lesions that erupted across the face and hands. Pustules on the inside of the mouth would bubble forth and singe their tongues. He would infect places and objects and the air itself. The affliction would divide and spread until all the corrupted souls were banished. Believers and pagans alike dreaded banishment itself more than the specter of rotting flesh.

Only those seemingly bestowed with divine guidance chanced returning to purity. One such soul was Naaman, the Syrian general who was desperate for a cure. The Mother once told us his story, admitting to its miraculous nature. This was when Elisha was the prophet of Israel, still eager to usurp the legacy of Elijah and so frail in his pride that he commanded two bears to devour more than forty boys outside of Bethel because a few of them jeered at his bald head. When Elisha heard of the afflicted general, he found a miracle worthy of his ambition and told the general by messenger to wash in the Jordan seven times and his flesh would thus be cleansed. Naaman wished to see the prophet whose hands coursed with God's might, but he was forced to hold faith in the prophet's words. For the general, words were paltry blunt things and yet he understood that God preferred to intervene in the fates of his followers through the medium of the unreal.

After Naaman was purified in the waters, the Mother ended her recounting. The patients were left with an apparent lesson in the curative force of faith. The veracity of holy signs. She did not recount how he offered to reward the prophet with silver after the general was cured. Elisha declined the gift but his servant Gehazi later told the general that his Master had changed his mind and asked for the silver. The general gladly paid him instead and Gehazi pocketed the money for himself. Elisha saw the entire exchange from the doorway of his home and infected the servant as punishment for his graft. The prophet then told him that all of his descendants shall likewise bear the affliction. The servant was fattening his herd on the gratitude of the cured soul, refashioning the prophet's words for his own avaricious ends.

Any word for the affliction partakes of the contagion it signifies and infects from house to house on rasping broken tongues. When the word is dismantled and its sound repeated a hundredfold, the mind relies on images to assuage its dissatisfaction. צרעת. The Hebrew word for the affliction. The word itself seems to contain condemnation with its hissing consonance. What it conjures originates from the innermost contours of the spirit and slowly stretches its tendrils throughout the flesh and indeed no region of the body's shell is impermeable to the snowy lesions. In Leviticus, it is a scab that must be uprooted by the priest of the tribe so that the noxious spirit may aerate. Two birds are brought into the tent of the afflicted. One bird slaughtered. The other preserved. Blood of the dead bird is admixed with water while the living bird is plunged into the water and lifted out. The priest drips the water upon the flesh of the afflicted. If the scabs are relinquished, the tribe reclaims the purified body and the dead bird is buried while the living one is tossed to the wind. Water is sloughed from the body of the afflicted, staining the sand.

The German word for the affliction, der Aussatz, is also the word for 'waste.' The substantive yearns to negate itself, literally describing a thing that is wrenched from utterance. The affliction located in the void of the word as it is located in the soul, or the void of the body. Named by a word that signifies the absence of speech. For Eckhart, words gain their power from the original Word, and thus contain the potential to conjure things. The Portuguese deem it morféia, from the Greek μορφη, which translates approximately as 'appearing form.' Implicit in this newly risen form is a transformative occurrence. A lesion is the mark of change upon the flesh and what occurs within the confines of the lesion may also change. A mutable form locatable upon a mutable surface. We have attempted to slow this doublefold transformation of flesh by instilling routine and sermonizing on the intransigence of the divine, the latter of which could be disputed with crude logic. We cannot refute time, no matter the proposed recalcitrance of our Maker, or the vociferousness of the prophet. As our bodies and the camp decayed, so did the ciphers of faith that conceal an eternal immutability.

No casket was fashioned and the office of the dead was whispered for fear the patients would hear us. Sister M. knelt on the floor kissing her beads. I stepped back against the wall still bearing the scent of damp oak newly splintered and covered half my face with the brim of my cornice. The form of the Mother's face was drawn of shadows writhing against the cloth and darkening down the length of her corpse as if it were slowly being pulled underwater so that the air trapped beneath the shroud wrestled for release.

At dusk we carried her up the rise to the weedless plot under the pecan trees where two bare wooden crosses stood. She would not fit inside the pit so we bent her legs back at the knees. We had expected storms throughout the day, but the sky was cloudless. The wind lifting off the water tasted of burnt cane. We each tossed a handful of dirt and muttered the song of Zachariah before Sister E. and I shoveled the mud back on top of her.

The patients gathered in the chapel for Mass save for Hans who was carried across the yard in a stretcher. A cloth was placed over his eyes to prevent the further flaring of his iritis, and his curved hands entwined on his belly. The women sat on the rear bench while the men sprawled beneath the altar on their own bench.

Although she rarely spoke, Sister E. possessed the most harmonious voice and read from John after which Sister M. stood up to tell the congregation of the Mother's death. The throathole from Han's failed tracheotomy spewed over his sheet while Lucas sat in the seamstress Louise's lap and grinded a pecan in his muddy fist. The patients had always claimed that graveyard pecans tasted sweetest. Perhaps the boy had already discovered the Mother's grave and gathered them on the weedless rise, or maybe he trailed us by listening to the rustle of our tunics, the straining of the twine that bound the corpse.

I passed hard tack to the able fingers and fed the rest by mouth while Sister E. poured the modest barrel of watery wine shipped upriver into a tin ladle. She walked among the congregation, crunching over the crumbs. Some of the men slurped the ladle dry and more wine was poured. Charles asked Sister M. if she were to be the new Mother, and she answered that we must now pray for the soul's ascent and concern ourselves later with camp matters. The boot on his left foot was spliced at the toes and leaking a yellow froth, which he kept wiping up with his hands.

He then asked Sister M. if she becomes the Mother, would she betray the word of John when he swore that God would cleanse us if we confessed our sins. The Mother, he said, taught us that sin was part of our souls and confession only frightened it, but God was waiting to wash it away. Sister M. said some will die with sin in their souls and they will keep dying until the sin drains away.

I escorted Ratherne and Cybele for the second Mass. Both of them were permitted by the Mother to house together in the third cabin because of their ancestry. Ratherne relied on one leg and had a patchwork of scars on his arms. Cybele's assuredly once handsome face slackened from a ruptured septum, and her gauze required changing every fortnight after her wounds reopened. I imagined that she would unravel it at night for her conjugal cabinmate, who pulled back the last strands of her hair, touching her face in both panic and splendor.

In the chapel, they listened dutifully to our incantations, and when I informed them of the Mother's death, Ratherne gently tapped his cane against the slats while Cybele pulled at her dress and shivered with faint prayers to the Virgin. The man spoke a patois of French that none but the Mother would venture to comprehend. Often he would say something in his rapid drawl and moments later

Cybele would beckon us near and speak. He lowered himself to the floor and kneeled on his good knee at the altar where a lithograph of the Resurrection was framed by candles.

For a thousand years those beset with the affliction were officially proclaimed dead. A mass was performed while they were alive, after which they were sent into the wilderness and given a bell and hooded robe sewn with holy insignia. If these souls approached a village or hamlet, they were commanded to ring the bell, which gave the unafflicted enough warning to rush indoors, or signaled horsemen to round up the pariah and return them to the wilderness.

Some villages allocated water and bread beside the path leading to their squares to avoid the mayhem that ensued upon the sound of the first peal, an easily recognizable sound for the bell given to them had a triangular tongue and produced a shrill timbre, quite different from the bell rung during the Mass in which their bodies were proclaimed dead. Perhaps a seething burgher was responsible for ringing the bell while the soul was led through the crowd, past mourning kin, to the open pit at the head of which stood a priest.

The afflicted, wearing a black veil, climbed into the pit as the priest flung three shovels of dirt onto the supplicant's back, intoning, Be dead to the world and reborn in God. Then the afflicted climbed from the pit and was exiled into the wilderness. After the banishment, the pit was filled and marked by a pauper's stone.

Like those who arrive at the camp, those beset with the affliction in previous centuries were divested of their name and legal rights, but a Mass does not mourn life's passing, it is rather the ritual of rebirth. Those who wandered into the desolate wood were reconstituted as errant souls, living ghosts who wished to avenge nothing, demanded no satisfaction, and who suffered hunger and abuse towards no supreme end. After their belongings and homes were incinerated, their families were condemned to a similar fate of earthly purgatory.

If one is officially proclaimed dead during their lifetime, then we have no record of their true death or burial, left to envision a corporal fate resolved by the scavenging of wolves and carrion. A lump in the middle of a field beset with maggots. Or perhaps, in a few exceptional cases, a wayfarer chanced upon the corpse and proceeded to bury it out of whatever remnant of piety they possessed, but many of afflicted souls walked headlong into a lake, or hurled themselves upon an outcropping of boulders. And yet others may have sufficiently hidden signs of infection, taken on another name, and returned to society once more, referring to their enigmatic past as a time of unholiness, worthy of nothing more than tacit bemusement.

The priest standing at the foot of the pit speaks for the township, the village council, and those austere fathers with their virgin brood. And when he speaks for the unafflicted, when he officiates the living death of the corrupt spirit kneeling below earth, he is simultaneously acknowledging the suffering, the loss of innocence, and the intrusion of evil that has befallen the newly dead. He acknowledges this evil because he summons it from that same village citizenry not solely during their confessions, but when witnessing the endlessly smoldering pyres, merchants with their egregious tax collections, the requisition of land from gentry proclaimed heretical. One could claim that the priest is vested with the authority to displace evil from one source and bestow it upon another. In this manner, the village is expurgated of sin, allowed to relish, if only until the next travesty, the illusion of innocence, which by fortuitous coincidence happens to be the priest's specialty. The citizenry has given the priest authority to judge between good and evil, so that they may be cleansed of sin and thus remain within the bounds of providence. The afflicted is stamped with evil by the priest's incantations, yet is also dispossessed of his soul, unmoored of evil and banished to the wood, thus returning to a state of innocence. We must not overlook what strain the priest must assume when he becomes this vessel of evil. He must carry it until the ritual requires him to dispel it upon a condemned soul, but the traces of the infectious substance remain with him after the pyres steam and the afflicted soul is traipsing miles away through a wintry hollow. Perhaps the residue of evil accounts in part for the weary brow of most priests, their haggard jowls, hairlines ever eclipsing regardless of whether they are fresh from seminary or puttering across chamber floors in their slippers and a silken robe.

Regarding these lowly men, one is reminded that sin is indeed a thief of youth. And perhaps these lingering traces of evil provide the motive for the former priest's nocturnal rambling. Listening to the confessions of the living dead and having nowhere to displace these tirades of helplessness but within his own beleaguered heart, set squarely away, gathering in mass and energy, dragging at his shoulders, slowly imploding his gut.

I shuddered at the foot of the rise that led to the pecan grove where an intricate rune drawn of milky ash stained the dirt.

The urge to laugh tugged my throat when I thought of the Mother who scorned slave magic throughout her life to now be consecrated under its spell. The rise seemed to scintillate in any gradation of light and perched at its crest was one of the cats that dwelled in the camp. A scion of Sister M.'s tabby and one of the feral males that preceded our arrival. The cat watched as I climbed the grove. It brandished little curiosity at my approach and turned toward another cat that was clawing the dirt of the Mother's plot. I attempted to frighten it by clapping, but it continued to dig and sniff at the earth until I gripped its nape and hoisted it upward. It opened its mouth in a silent hiss and flailed its claws languorously until I tossed the creature down to let it wander off and join its partner.

After the patients had been served their breakfast of tack and pea soup, a young man dressed in a waistcoat was calling at the gate. He removed his hat and nervously informed us of the doctor's arrival. The tugboat was docked some hundred yards downriver for the pilot was superstitious of docking within sight of the camp. We followed the young man to the tugboat where the doctor was unloading freight while the pilot remained at the bow.

The doctor did not readily introduce himself to us, seemingly more concerned that we might drop his enshrouded glass bowls, which he claimed held reptilian species. He wore a widebrimmed hat that darkened his smooth face. The tugboat remained docked while we carried boxes of his equipment and belongings to the scullery at the rear of the house where the previous doctor had established his quarters and examination room. The room had been unoccupied since last fall and the floor was speckled with motes of dust and cat feces. The doctor was evidently perturbed by the scullery's condition and said he was not lodging his belongings there until it was thoroughly washed.

Some of the patients wandered from their cabins and gathered beyond the loggia to await the doctor should he emerge from the house. When Sister M. instructed them to return to their cabins, Charles said to tell the doctor that Hans was dying, but she was adamant that they leave the yard. While I stacked trays in the men's cabin, I watched Lucas rolling a marble over the discolored arm of Hans while he looked to be fretlessly sleeping. All but his head and right arm were tucked into the cot. His wheezing had quieted since last I saw him.

Although the rains had quit since late morning, the roof

was still leaking, and rot had encircled the center of the floor. During dinner I informed Sister M. of the leak and she told me to inquire whether Charles could climb to the roof and refasten the burlap covering in the morning. She then spoke of assisting the doctor while he tended to Hans. Unlike the previous doctor, she said, the newly arrived one was rather careless in his treatment. He was given to episodes where he appeared absentminded with the instruments. As he widened the incision in the throat, he seemed to alternate between a gay humming and speaking to himself not about the surgery he was attending to, but about the weather, or the names of varied foliage he had seen in the camp's domain. Sister M. said that before inserting the rubber cylinder into Hans' throat, the doctor washed his hands at the basin, proceeded to his desk where he jotted down a few sentences, and fed one of his lizards an ant he picked from a glass jar. He was nonetheless polite in his requests, she said, and prepared coffee for them both, an amenity he had brought upriver.

One abiding tendency of camp life, besides the perilous summer rain, has been the precarious presence of both doctors and priests. The Mother, who resided here since the camp's inception, counted three priests and two doctors during her tenure. Both were not required by their respective institutions to reside on the grounds. The previous doctor resided in the scullery but left after the first summer. He was a rather humorless man, a characteristic seeming to befit many servants of disease. For him, the patients were piles of rot strung together by necrotic bones and bedecked with a meshwork of calloused nerves. He worked alone and abstained from surgery as much as possible.

Priests, however, acted unsurprisingly more anxious than doctors when confronted with a permanence of place. This restlessness is particular to the priests of this nation, as if all men of God wish to be circuit riders calling farmers to testify while women swoon to the cadence of their words, riding from town to town with their good book as sole possession, and leaving each town before civic adoration becomes spite.

The last priest was admired by the patients, but we believed that he patronized them, tapping their heads in the manner one would a family hound, and the tone of his voice rose to an embarrassing lilt when he held their hands and dripped water upon them with an indolent grin. Rarely would he dine with us. He preferred his food brought to the chapel where he lodged, pulling out his cot and pillow and blanket from beneath the altar. The patients gossiped about the priest's wanderings at night, which probably occurred while we ate dinner or read to one another in the parlor. One patient, who had long since absconded, told of calling for the priest from the stoop of the men's cabin because a patient within wished to confess, but the priest was oblivious, pensively eyeing the ground with his arms folded behind his back.

A mallow picked from the riverline curled from a tin cup on my desk. Combing the edge at dawn before terce prayer brought beauty of little consequence. If I revealed each of my transgressions in these pages, what would I confess to in my hurried hours? A black ant clung to one of the pink petals, aggravated by dust. I scraped at mud to uproot the flower and tossed all but its radiant heart into the water before I beheaded the last of our fowl and gave the kitchen a thorough scrubbing. When I put on my nightshirt and pulled back the counterpane, my restlessness surged with the rising riverline, and I sat down to apprehend my thoughts, beholden to the soporific spell of words inscribed.

If I were so fortunate as to visit my lines during the day, I would recoil helplessly before memories I thought had vanished since residing at camp. Feckless pathways of an unmarried yet virtuous creature who ponders store windows and gently admires yet ultimately rebukes the sweaty assault of passing strangers who offer to purchase whatever lustrous species beckons beneath the glass.

Behind my nails bred flesh and dirt and water. Ink stained my fingertips. A witness of banishment who testified to the tedium of camplife to induce sleep. For its narcoleptic effect do I owe my gratitude to writing, otherwise I consider it a propagation of gossip, a shameless exercise in onanism, nourished by a delusory fixation with posterity. Perhaps I should better expend this impulse towards the construction of romance novels so much adored in my prehistory. Yet I would hoard those pages as well. Each word inscribed for naught.

When first lying down to sleep, I fashioned a romance in my mind, an epic yarn of intrigue and infamy, and yet I fell asleep before the opening paragraphs were fully composed. In the succeeding night, as I lay down again, I tried to recall the opening paragraphs from the previous night, but I fell asleep before creating any characters or episodes or pithy maxims through which my setting could unfold. So it continued with each night, a romance hardly begun, or which endlessly repeated its own preamble like the victrola only repeating an orchestral introduction, teasing our ears with the promise of wondrous sound before the needle retraces itself to the opening bars.

Most of my patience had been devoted to camplife, and I had little left over for the construction of fantasy. I fell asleep so quickly because I sliced pages with my nail file, creased the bindings of my daybook, and began to transcribe unholy minutia. I could imagine both a perilous, foolish world and remain faithful to how my days were spent, or if I had more leisurely hours, perhaps both would be possible, but then I would sacrifice my unspoken vows to the Order, and be reduced to vagrancy, scavenging after scraps of food instead of a satisfying adjective.

I wish to imagine the language of birds inscribed upon the scene, not the ghostly drone pouring from the victrola that was propped on a chair and cranked by Louise while the doctor stood in the wet grass, calling each patient to walk the path that cut between the men's and women's cabins. When Ratherne was called upon to walk, Cybele led him to the path, averting her eyes from the doctor. She had refused bandaging the last fortnight, declining the offer of both Sister E. and myself. Her dressing was almost fully stained and had begun to unspool from the crown of her head. While walking, Louise stopped in the middle of the path and nearly swooned. I called Lucas to bring her to the cabin and when he returned he took her place cranking the phonograph. The sergeant and Este, the two wheelchair-bound patients, played blackjack with Charles, who waited till he had finished his cigarette before stiffly sauntering down the path with his hands in his pockets while the sergeant whistled at him over the music and Este lifted the cards left facedown on the stoop.

After his observations were completed, the doctor asked me to retrieve the victrola from Lucas who heard me approaching and spun the crank more quickly, grinning at the sound of the feverish voices and the scratching needle. Walking back to the scullery, I saw Sister E. sitting beside Hans beneath the oak and the shadows of the branches had joined together as the clouds signaled rain. Before taking lunch in the house, the doctor assigned me the task of transcribing the notes he had made during his observations into one of his leatherbound journals, which was stacked beside a handbook of dermatology, some monographs on eye diseases, a collection of Jacobean comedies and volumes of Paracelsus and Bartram.

I rendered the sometimes nearly inscrutable chains of words into terse sentences of blue ink. He wrote of the 'profound alienation' of patients from their own bodily decay, and that a sentient form that fails to interpret stimuli is 'further subject to the whims of nature.' He listed the actions in which this alienation is discerned and beside the phrase 'repercussions on psychic life,' he scrawled a question mark. He acknowledged that since Charles does not limp, he must not register pain. 'Because he walks thus,' he wrote, 'his foot can never heal itself.' Lucas' near blindness was a similar case.

He acknowledged that the boy's gaze did not shirk away from the sun even if its brightness burned his eyes. Under these admissions, he drew a series of human figures steadily declining from a ready stance to an infantile crawl. The period of time denoted for this degeneration could span many years or occur within a fortnight.

I redrew the ailing bodies, shading the limbs, adding noses, hair, eyes, giving each face a serene expression. Perhaps the faces I drew suggest that I agreed with the doctor's theory of 'alienation from decay,' and my sketches were the work of a deluded caricaturist portraying intoxicants of divinity who imbibed fairytales to soothe their ruinous hours.

At midnight I was awoken by the screams of cats copulating and fighting just outside the southwing in a stretch of grass shielded by oaks where one may find in the morning hours tangled tufts of hair and shredded leaves encrusted with blood. Their wails would usually last until each female of the pack had been ravished and each male had been gouged, save for the victorious one who sauntered off, followed by his beleaguered horde. Each year the orgy became fiercer, sustaining itself on more bloodshed, the cats themselves becoming less timid among us. Fortified by their multitude, they scavenged the cabins and stables and slipped into the house to claw at the cabinets and topple jars from their shelves. During those nights, Sister M. awoke when her tabby cried from the floor, begging her mistress to be allowed atop the bed and protected from the trespass of tomcats.

Suffering lurked in my bedchamber hours. Shadows encased in shadows bearing visions of bodies undergoing prolonged liquefaction with arms outstretched to the merciless sky. Decomposing hands tearing at faces that melded to the fingers and slid down the arms and torso. Layers of flesh unpeeled, revealing more layers as if the flesh were impelled to spawn as it was being ripped away. Again my eyes startled open to sounds of screaming, and I was unsure whether it issued from the cats outside, or transpired from the melting mouths that appeared in the dream.

I carried the doctor's lunch to the scullery. Pushing back the door with my foot, the room was empty, and I set the tray on his desk. For all the visits and commotion that had occurred there, I marveled at how odorless and perfectly still it was until I heard a faint whistle and turned to see Lucas in the dooryard, tonguing his gapped tooth and shaking the marbles in his pocket. He gestured for me to follow him and scurried toward the rise, dipping eastward into the high grass with his hands splayed out to gauge a path. He clutched the tips of the grass and pulled them down as he kneeled by the woodline.

I lifted my habit and underskirt. Moths swarmed against my legs. The copper wings of dragonflies floated over the path. Brush unfolded until the path ended in more tall grass and torn branches.

My face was burning with sweat, and I wiped it with my damp sleeve. The heat was mocking my clumsy vestments. Occasionally the path would dip into mud, and the coolness crept up my stockings. I climbed through ditch vine, wrenching my habit from thorns. The smell of muskrat spread through the moss, less officious than skunkspray, more like the heavy odor of the foreman's son who leaned against us while we spun the mule. The rows of machines produced such a din that I could feel his breath and the touch of his lips on my neck, but gratefully I could not hear what he said. The other girls and I would laugh in the alley while imagining the substance of his words, but I never spoke of the grip of his nails above my hips, or when he would slide his limp palm across my thigh while I kicked the pedal.

Steam lifted from the clearing, and the doctor stepped softly through pools of night rain already brought to a bubbling stench. He orbited each trunk, placed one hand on the bark while his other held a burlap sack, carefully stepping so as not to splash and alert his prey. At intervals the shifting steam concealed him, so he suddenly would be transported to another tree when the veil passed, the brim of his hat tilted towards the canopy.

He peeled what must have been lizards from the bark. I imagined their bulbous eyes flinching as he seized their necks before he paused again for light to strike wood and herald his catch. At the bottom of the sack, the lizards must have writhed as a tangled mass before each fell limp with exhaustion, tonguing the rough sheath while their bearer pranced in his grimy coat, sometimes hesitating to seize them in favor of studying their calibrations upon the wood, or awaiting the arrival of brethren to gorge his sack.

The Mother had told us that before the War the camp was a plantation owned by a General reputed to have on occasion invited his garrison from downriver to partake of drunken ribaldry with a wagonload of prostitutes. The General's wife took to her tonic baths during these orgiastic weekends when the soldiers would strip the prostitutes and chase them into the woods whereupon they rounded them up with rifles held aloft and suspenders unstrapped, parading the grounds unaware of the merciless defeat they would soon encounter. Fireworks rocketed over the canopy, illuminating the women as they scrambled through the brush.

As is true with most strategists of combat, the General was a student of history and chose the tract of land because it was the site of a conquered tribe. When the rebel flag was raised for morning reveille, the barbarian lineage of the land was further expunged, but when he returned to his home after the War, he found the rooms ransacked and canefields burned. All but one of his eight and thirty slaves had abandoned the plantation. The last to remain was a decrepit stablehand he purchased in the city for three dollars who was too senile to believe in his freedom. All the horses had been stolen and the stablehand was shoeless, foraging in the woods with a sprawling white beard.

The General's wife was plagued by feverish episodes and

unable to rest. Her husband suspected syphilis and considered admitting her to the hospital but stubbornly held onto his home for a decade longer, sitting on the porch during the crop season where he scrawled letters to comrades banished like himself or polished his rifles for the twilight hunt or spooled his line for angling. His wife often sat beside him silently rocking and draped in netting. When the riverboats bustling with carpetbaggers drifted by, they must have stared at the old couple sitting on the porch with both fascination and contempt. The man wearing riding boots and a creased medaled uniform beside the enshrouded catatonic woman.

In the dead season, he dragged piles of kindling into the parlor and axed them before the fireplace. At night he wrote more letters. Some folded away in his desk without ever bearing an address. Every morning he raised the rebel flag until a barge of bluecoats came ashore and pistolwhipped him to the cusp of consciousness whereupon he ordered his stablehand to lower and furl the flag.

The camp was founded on some three hundred acres of mostly swampland, the southeastern border of which nudged against a small town. The purpose of the camp was initially concealed from the townspeople or anyone who lived within a halfday's journey of the front gate. Officially, the newly acquired land was to be used for ostrich breeding, but the townspeople were immediately incredulous and soon a poacher who had wandered unseen among the camp relayed to the townspeople what he had seen and some landowners further down the meander resolved to burn the camp and bury its ashes in the river.

In the front desk, beside the whittling knife and inkjar, was a map Sister M. told us not to unroll and remove from the parlor drawer. On it, the river flowed downward past towns all buried in the bend, stationed in another realm. Some names were stained and illegible. The seal of an eagle was stamped on the edge of the map and signed Capt. Allen Jumel, 1881. Beside the map was an article cut from the town's newspaper and framed in glass.

On the night of February 16th, citizens from the neighboring town alongside parish authorities endeavored to wage war against the new colony.

The parish has already refused to sell bread or other supplies to the colony and the nurses and servants on staff have been warned in print that they will be shot if they should exit the grounds.

A tally at the scene recorded three-dozen men armed with a variety of weapons: shotguns, caneblades, torches, and rope. The mob erupted in a fearsome chant outside the gates, threatening to raid the colony unless all of its tenants left immediately. They claimed it resided too close to the river and that its rages and debris would infect their own domiciles. After the chants subsided and the temperature fell, the mob dispersed, having burnt the postbox at the colony's entrance.

When I heard the Mother tell of her experience during that night, I wondered if she truly did remain inside the front parlor patching trousers for a patient, or if the patients had stirred from their cots, fully expecting to be chased into the swamp, lucky to make it twenty yards before the dogs had enclosed them and the guns were leveled. And perhaps no one in the camp had the slightest trepidation because they knew the mob feared contagion much more than the proximity of the camp. Perhaps a patient who has since died or escaped crossed the grounds and saw the flamelit bodies jostling against the gate beneath a cloud of steam. Or maybe the dogs were already on the grounds, encircling the house and the cabins, charging through the soilbeds while the stable erupted with frantic wings. As the Mother told it, the chants soon dissolved into a loud exchange of opprobrium and lamentation and the mob eventually vanished with the exception of a few men muttering and pacing beneath torches nearly extinguished.

As we committed our faculties to the alleviation of suffering, the patients were bound by law to imbibe their suffering until either their souls were freed, or the law deemed them purified, which entailed dormancy of affliction, or a lack of newly appearing signs over a suitable swath of time. Admitting in their faithless hours that the affliction was incurable, the patients could disregard time as an absolute. They were no longer waiting as they did before their banishment when their fate was undetermined and thus more burdensome and expectations nursed them to struggle for dignity and battle thereafter to assume it as their own.

The burden of time drifted ethereally into mere adornments of reasoning, and the interminable drought of expectation pacified them. Banishment atrophies all recollections of exterior living. All codes and petty stupefactions and riotous bustling that the outer world is privy to eventually dissolve. Any habits or ambitions that would profit them in the confines of exterior living had been rendered as useless as their mitten hands. I still confront with pitiless horror the thought of anyone who had dwelled at camp returning to the city wharves and calling after dock work or opening the door of a past abode to find another family sitting to dinner.

I laid down no vows, wed myself to no institution, and my duties were left unwritten. I may have been untethered, a demiurge of my own volition, but I expected no deliverance from camp. Since my arrival, when I first kissed the Mother's hand and made introductory rounds of the cabins, I fancied no other cast of fate even if residing at camp had heightened my experience of pain, each quiver of muscle or twitching tooth signaled my fixation. I approached pain timidly before dreaming of perforating it and emerging on the other side to rediscover that pain resists change of intensity in favor of altering its rhythm or location, which is not dissimilar from blood traversing the body at varied intervals and intensities while its volume remains unchanged.

Pain was an errant fluid that may in the morning swarm the spine when attending to the bedridden and in the afternoon cloud the brain with searing eruptions while at night coldly possessing the bones of my fingers gripping the pen. The eradication of any desire to request an end to my tenure did not arise from a sense of belonging to the camp. The aspirations of the city officials were hollow from the beginning, founded on the belief that, for the damned, any prison is a form of refuge. Like those patients who did not escape the camp although their bodies permitted it, my residence also deepened my loathing of the outer world. Our fortress without walls quelled any desire to return and any faith that the outer world would welcome us again.

The stockaded fatalist Jeremiah told the Lord he could not speak for he was a child, prone to enter heaven by his very essence. The Lord replied He would put the words in the prophet's mouth. The Savior declared one must be born again and become as a little child to enter the Kingdom of Heaven.

To reside in camp was likewise to be born again and rendered childlike. Perhaps this lends seemliness to the former doctor's ready condescension before his patients. When one is admitted to camp, the inaugural rite involved the act of renaming. Some were unable to name themselves during their first days in the camp, either from indifference at being named or disbelief they had truly arrived. The Mother then named such cases after their corresponding saintday. Some had chosen a name for themselves and we never inquired after the name's significance. And the name remained. They called out this name when submerged in fever throes. When post was sent to or from camp, this name was written on it. Patients who returned either forcibly or willfully claimed they used this name in the exterior and would not answer to those who persisted in using the name attending to their first birth.

St. Vincent instructed his Sisters to abandon their homes when attending to the sick, a state of homelessness that produces langnor, as in St. Augustine's sentiment, ipse est langnor meus, which causes one to seek more fervently the presence of the divine. The act of prayer for His homeless servants is achieved through attending to the sick, which in turn enacts the purification of sin. In my possession I have two proofs of an existence preceding my arrival.

The first proof is a letter sent to me by my great aunt in which she describes how both her household and her town have become more dissolute. Fearful weather. Dead husband. Thankless children. Jobs vanished. Lawless mayor. Fallen porch. Spells. She wondered whether I remembered the last time we saw each other, and I failed to remember ever seeing her while the address on the envelope was of a place utterly foreign to me.

The second proof is a vial of green glass with the date 1866 marked on the bottom. I found it in my vestment one night after I had returned to my bedroom when I worked in an infirmary up North. A patient must have slipped it in my pocket while I was on my final round of the floor. The interior of the vial was odorless and attached to the cork was the frailest metal chain bedecked with the cross of St. James. The chain has long since broken, but I sewed the cross beneath the opening of my left sleeve. The morning after my discovery, I inquired in the records whether a patient had deceased during the night. 3, deceased. 1, discharged.

If attending to the sick is a form of prayer, what would the corresponding act be, what do the sick enact by being sick? Does the helplessness, the suffering they undergo take the form of a rejoinder to prayer, issuing from that immutable, austere force, the duration of breath exhaled before the deluge of more words? Perhaps a faithful attendant should regard sickness as an end in itself, yet one cannot help but assume the sick embody an aspect of the divine, since prayer is manifested through caregiving. Based on the severity of the affliction, one would assume heaven to be righteously indignant, festering with guile and invective. They have been smothered by the same wrath that struck the Egyptians, and they must wonder why they have been chosen to transmit such signs, asking themselves what transgression they have committed to be burdened with this nameless disease.

One of the duties St. Vincent neglected to stipulate, and which I tried to carry out while residing at camp, necessitates convincing the patients that though they may indeed be witnesses to evil, their souls remain impermeable unless they allow this earthly affliction to pierce their innermost being. My assurances reeked of the doctrine of renunciation, the old stimulant beloved by many a sisterly servant. For what was I telling them but a core of virtue resides within, and this core may remain untarnished by both their own affliction and the wrath of man? Yet how can a soul remain unblemished after these ravages have been delivered? Perhaps the clergy of yesteryear were right in declaring the affliction a disease that spreads to the soul.

What God would stipulate the contemplation of suffering as an acknowledged form of devotion? Is it because suffering foments profound doubt in divine will and God would have us endlessly doubting to bolster our faith and strengthen our devotion? Or is it once we confront suffering as an essential condition of being, we will cling more desperately to our faith as a refuge of the dispirited? I could never consider my camp duties as exercises of devotion. I preferred to let the hours guide me. The duties were too numerous to list. They melded together into one prolonged spell in which I was distracted from the curious task set before me of tending to the same dissolute world that I urged the patients to renounce with the promise of salvation.

Some mornings I awoke and felt like the malefactor on the left side of Christ, condemned, expecting salvation without trial, and the next morning I was the malefactor on the right side, also condemned, yet cowering in humble obedience, asking to be remembered in eternity. Other mornings I would startle awake among a crowd of soldiers and magistrates on a hilltop, jeering at the morning spectacle.

Since Ratherne arrived in the camp, three markings appeared on the graves of the newly buried. Two afflicted souls and the Mother. When I surprised Cybele at dusk with my bandaging box, she agreed to redressing as if solely to be rid of me.

Ratherne was in the corner of the cabin, sitting in a pile of shavings with a dull hunting knife and various lengths of wood. I began to unwrap Cybele's stained ribbons and asked Ratherne what he was making. She translated his answer and said he was building a place to sit. After each breath, she swallowed more mucus. The gauze stuck to her abscesses, and I sprinkled water on it and peeled it away carefully, unveiling swollen eyes clouded with pus. Her arms hung over the cot and her breath issued in acrid streams from her septum. Of her own accord she says nothing, yet if she is directed a question, she answers forthrightly. I had assumed since seeing the last marking in the plot of the Mother, that Ratherne was aided by his cabinmate. I asked Cybele if she had visited the pecan grove, and she replied that she had gone there on occasion to escape the confines of the cabin. I asked her about the markings on the Mother's plot when I daubed at hardened bits of pus with a sponge. She winced when her tongue tasted the clotted drip of her nose. Ratherne stopped carving and heaved himself up to open the suitcase beside his cot, retrieving a pipe hewn of dark wood. He stood beside the door and lit it.

I rewound the dressing for fear it was too tight against her abscesses. Cybele said the markings are made to tell God where the souls are. If He must look longer for them, she said, He gets mad and sends more sickness.

I made a space in the dressing for her eyes and pinned it back so that her hair could flow freely. Ratherne reached for a clump of stained bandage and set it aflame with a match, letting it burn in his hand before tossing it into the yard.

I awoke with a parched throat, the scent of wax still lingering in my chamber. From the landing, I could see the parlor door still ajar. After I descended the stairs, I found Sister M. asleep at her desk with no letter or open book beneath her arm. She had a calm face but her fingers trembled slightly and her vestment seemed to constrict her breathing. Cats had yet to arrive in the yard. Moonlight cut across the chimes of the broken clock hanging on the wall, but the river buried its reflection.

The Mother told us that the natives believed the river's source was in the underworld. She recited a myth about a chief who was in mourning for his wife. While he fasted alone in his tepee, he was addressed by a spirit of the dead who told him that he would be shown a path to the underworld where he could gaze upon his wife if he promised never to speak of the path thereafter. The chief agreed, and the spirit guided him on a long journey to see his wife, and once he set his eyes upon her, the spirit filled the path with clouded waters.

For the natives of the riverbank, the pathway to the underworld ran counter to the river's course. The chief's longing resisted the flow of time, and the tributaries were formed by other lovers who faltered in their longing, who broached a course that ran aground, or plunged into a tidal lake. The chief must have known he had arrived in the underworld for the desolate stretch that surrounded him did not resemble the land described in those other misguided journeys. He knew he had arrived because the spirit had led him there. This hell does not resemble the one imagined by Adam in that blind puritan's exhausting poem as 'sad, dark, noisome...A lazar-house wherein were laid numbers of all diseased, all maladies.' Standing beside the window, I could not envision a waterless pathway veering against time. As it poured onward, I saw the waters stifle each break of light as the edges of the yard flowed seamlessly with a current that led to neither heaven nor hell, but drained into a tepid sea, dragging with it all the tokens of banishment.

When I tapped Sister M.'s shoulder, she told me she was watching the front grounds, and that she would retire soon. I lifted the lantern and placed it on the parlor table, further from her trembling hand. She told me to go back upstairs and turned her head toward the center window, still resting it on her arm.

Because she resented the flattery Charles bestowed on Sister E., she suspected that he was the one stealing supplies. By dozing in the parlor, she was seeking evidence against him. I had always wanted to believe that she herself was guilty of thievery, partly accounting her vociferous accusations against Charles, but I could not fathom her plying such cunningness. Somewhere she would falter, or plead for redemption as she dabbed a cake crumb from her tunic. Sister E. could not be the thief either. She had the hunger of a motherless fawn, that is, she imbibed her morsels solely to prolong her prayers, and her immutable weight perfectly filled her gown whereas mine ballooned over my hips.

I had never glimpsed anyone but Paul on the grounds at that late hour, and he was also known by his cabinmates to wander the camp, hunting for muskrat and toad, or stringing fish from the river. Which prisoner, if permitted by his jailer, would not venture out on nightly walks and imagine in the darkness that the confines of his walking spread further out while the fragile quietness allowed for the pretense of solitude? It could be poorly argued that a true prisoner is never afforded such privileges because strolling at night may curb pensive restlessness, induce a more vigorous sense of autonomy that being confined to a bed would not. The nightwalk had been a recurring pastime among those who resided at the camp, and perhaps this precluded them from claiming true imprisonment. Perhaps because of the diminished severity of our own confinement as sisters, we were not known to steal away from the house at night. We would shed our tunics as exhaustion lay heavy in folds of fat, our bolted door sufficing for any desirable illusion of solitude.

Every night sojourner had his purpose. Paul went to hunt, Ratherne to go discover whether the dirt was evil, and Charles, according to Sister M., was out thieving supplies from the house. But what of the priest, the one who slept on the chapel cot, what was he searching for on his nightly walks? Was he also drawing in the dirt to see if it were evil, or stumbling through hyacinth, asking his paltry savior which way to the city, pattering barefoot on the banks with parish priests and bishops in his mind whom he would like to inquisition, preferably without fire, but in a cell with cackling birds. Maybe it was during one of these excursions that the last priest flagged a boat downriver and when he arrived to report to the bishop, he spoke of airless rooms infested with disease, a ramshackle chapel sinking into a swamp while the ungrateful nunnery traded verses in their mansion. If his report spread among the parishes, then all the clergy would have absolved their names from consideration and only those fathers who owe penance to the bishop would ever be assigned here. But for hierarchies to prune their ranks, exterior forces must prompt them and what force could dare breach the vault of heaven? I expected a fatherless keep for at least until the end of spring, regardless of whatever solace the bishop wished to offer.

The missing supplies coincided with the arrival of the two new patients to the women's cabin, who arrived together from the holding terminal. Through their shared confinement, they fostered mutual reliance and disdain. In the camp they were known as the grandmother and the girl, but the grandmother was hardly ten years older than Louise, and the girl was around twenty years of age.

They bedded on opposite corners and rarely spoke to one another in the evenings yet during the days both of them tended to the garden behind their cabin. The girl was plagued with breathing difficulties, but her hands were nimble and attentive among the crops. Occasionally her lesions flared up if she were beneath the sun for too long. The grandmother hobbled among the wet mounds, pausing to scrape vermin with her cane. She boiled vegetables for the other patients and supplied water from the pump beside the river.

She was known as the grandmother not solely because of her accelerated state of decay, but also because of her motherly generosity towards the other patients. Other than Louise, the only other resident of the woman's cabin was Lucas, but if he were to be considered a resident, he was a shiftless one, wandering as he did past the rut gouged between both cabins.

For many a patient each day was without regiment save for the three meals that bracketed their long convalescence. Not one patient shared the same daily pattern, but feeding forced their rhythms to intersect and ensured that their movements would orbit closer to their cabins as conversation became a set of mangled curses against hunger. After each meal was consumed, they remained inside, napping or reading until their dexterity replenished and they arose to return to the yard. Tasks were rarely assigned, but most plied some craft or exhibited preference toward certain labor. However, the men mostly spat or smoked in the shade, having long ago exhausted yarns of their randy exploits before arrival.

Days were pummeled and sieved. Discipline was practiced in lieu of charity. Each name would be relinquished, each wound sutured and gleaming. Their lanterns dimmed and we dwelled earnestly over our pages in an effort to relieve our feet of burden and ward their presence from our thoughts. Yet whatever chatter filled those moments almost exclusively concerned their fate: necessary repairs to walkways and roofs and floors as if talk itself could rid us of ruin, as if talk could fortify us and instruct our hands in the rudiments of carpentry, the craft upon which our faith was established, so a larger chapel could be built which would preserve a silence to outlive us and testify to our inheritors how much we strove, how vast our passion unfurled, whether we could see such tasks to their end, or if our residence at the camp would suffocate all ambition.

When the cabins were utterly ramshackle, the patients were scattered upstairs, each to his own chamber, furnished with bell and cot while the Mother housed in what is now Sister E.'s chamber, and the other sisters bedded in the parlor, one of whom was Sister M. who probably resented crowded quarters and always being at the patients' beckoning, hearing their feverish rants while she shuffled through memories of her former life to ease into sleep. She must have been grateful that some separation, however indistinct, now prevented casual summoning, or her having to hear murmurs betwixt walls, or clean up bedpans spilt over the floors. Instead, she sprawled in her matriarchal throne, draped in luscious netting and coiled beside her sphinx.

Since the patients were allowed to travel to the camp with but few possessions, the cabins appeared sparse from within. The possessions they took with them seemed swept into the far reaches of the floor, tucked behind the oven, or propped above the rafters, but the objects were indeed in plain sight if one's eyes pierced the emptiness of the room. Cybele's oak comb with the brass prongs. Or her medallion with the sullied engraving. Talismans hovered near those bodies that preserved their force. Lacquered case of epaulettes. Book of hymns. A cane hanging from a nail. A linen pouch of marbles. Stacks of letters saved from a fire ignited by deputies. Bridal veil. Framed photograph of a family posing before a backdrop at a county parade. Deck of cards bearing illustrations of nymphs in flowering jungles. A hunting knife. More wilted letters, calendars, postcards. Pocket watch. Chain necklace attached to a locket. Pair of velvet riding gloves.

Some objects, like Louise's leather valise, could remain apart from their owner, but their owner's eyes lingered towards their presence, and that is how the molded floor of the cabin emerged from emptiness into a crowded stage of vigilance and jealousy and agitation. Each object was bound to its place by a sacred arrangement, which prompted recollection and afforded them respite from the amnesia that had bleached their former lives. For as their bodies rested while they resided at camp, their memory degenerated. A premature senility overcame them and attending to their talismans permitted them clarity, as if they possessed the magic of a priest or sorcerer who fluidly traversed both past and future, but who returned to the present as a vanquished spirit.

Este conveyed fewer possessions to the camp than any other patient. He was an apprentice pharmacist in a Texas border town who was apprehended after lesions on his hand alarmed his employer. After the local hospital forced him out, he was transported by boxcar into Oklahoma, which also refused to treat him, whereupon he crisscrossed the borders of more than half a dozen states. When the train stopped in the railyards, the conductor was instructed to feed and wash him through the slats in the car while still being responsible for delivering the train's usual cargo. However, in some states, the conductor could not unload the cargo because the stationmaster would not allow the train to dock.

By the time a telegram confirmed that the holding terminal could receive him, he was somewhere in Missouri, huddled beneath hay on the floor of the car, sleepless in anticipation of the horn signaling another railyard where the haulers of cargo would gather around the car, whistling and throwing food through the slats and the conductor would slip the hose nozzle inside and spray him down. As the train continued to another state, he would strip naked of his soaked clothes and hold them outside the car so the wind could dry them. When he arrived in the city, he was malnourished and feverish. The lesions on his hands had become infected, and he was experiencing the onset of rickets. He had ridden through the country in the throes of unimaginable pain, and he discovered that the country was a land of limitless night.

He told his prehistory to the sergeant after losing all his money and cigarettes to him in a bet, and the two of them finished the whiskey the sergeant had brought with him from the city, the empty flask of which has since become a talisman of the men's cabin. Because no one else asked Estes directly about his prehistory, the contours and digressions that belong to it were left to whoever decided to tell it, thus the story sometimes had fanciful or improbable variations.

My version has been culled and rarefied from the multiple versions heard by other patients. I included the detail about him being a pharmacist's assistant because I have seen the apron he wore when the health officials and police apprehended him at work. After he identified himself in the pharmacy, they led him in handcuffs out into the street where they locked him inside a cage draped in canvas and bolted to a carriage bed.

The chapel attached to the hospital up north where I worked owned a large Bible that contained more than a hundred prints depicting various encounters with the corresponding verse beneath them. The Bible's rightful place was atop the lectern, but during the evenings, when I took a break from my rounds, I sometimes carried it to the front pew and opened it on my lap. I took the brief time I had with the book to peruse the prints before its bulk tired my legs. Some were admittedly tawdry while others enchanted me.

One particularly enchanting print depicted Job sitting in the desert, stricken by boils and banished from his village. A few paces away from him were three of his friends who had traveled from their respective villages, each seized by a posture of lamentation.

They sat with their friend for seven days and nights until he finally spoke of the evil that God had allowed to be cast upon him. What both captivated and alarmed me most about the print was the disparity between Job's stricken flesh and the smooth, radiant flesh of his companions. Looking at the once seamless form now fragmented by boils that covered every inch of it made me uneasy so that my eyes drifted across the page to the arid mountains in the background veiled by the dust that the others had tossed above their heads in despair. Perhaps it was not the broken form of his body that horrified me, but the expression of profound irresolution on his face, not of the unwavering faith we would typically assume. But this irresolution was conveyed through a taciturn, yet fixated guise, as if he were waiting for a hare to emerge from its burrow so he could pummel its skull with a rock.

We are never told whether Job had the affliction or not. All we are given are signs, and, as Heraclitus writes, God neither declares or hides, he sets forth by signs. Before displaying signs of affliction, Job had lost all of his livestock and children. As he sat in ashes and scraped the boils off his flesh with a pottery shard, his wife tried to convince him to forsake his faith by cursing God and he asked her: Shall we receive good at the hand of God, and shall we not receive evil? Satan had to spare Job's life, but the evil sent to him could approach its unfathomable limits. Yet after the affliction strikes Job, Satan's curses are exhausted, leaving us to infer from Satan's reprieve that the affliction is the most severe curse that may be delivered upon us, excluding death itself unless of course death were to arrive after infection.

After his desert exile, Job's health was restored, his livestock replenished, and his name continued through new offspring. The magnitude of his trial dwindles to a mere bout of indigestion when contrasted with the experiences of the afflicted, but understanding this will heal no one. Perhaps all it can do is partly explain how hitherto lawful citizens could transform into gamblers, liars, philanderers and thieves upon being marked and banished, many of them knowing fully that they will not live long enough like Job to see generations of their offspring pass before them. Most of them will not be rewarded in this life for exercising faith through their banishment, regardless of the tenacity of their belief, or the pitch of their lamentations. They may feebly grip a priest's hand while nearing death, but they will most likely never speak to God. In their futile scramble for earthly salvation, their faith will not subside. Perhaps there are days when the afflicted feel disemboweled of grace, the expressions on their faces resembling the dispossessed stare of Job, undaunted by death yet perplexed by the apparent absence of God. No companions have arrived to lament their fates with crouched postures in the swamp. Their spouses have in most cases abandoned them after confronting the likelihood of never seeing them again.

Beneath the image were printed two questions that Job asked during his monologue, 'If I be wicked, why then labor I in vain? If I wash myself with snow water, and make my hands never so clean?' These questions culminate in his oblique prophecy of the Son, in which he admits to bearing anger against the otherworldliness of God, and that no figure like Hermes stands as arbiter between heaven and earth. He contemplates his stricken palms while the other three quietly writhe behind him, more in dread of being cursed themselves than in righteous concern for their friend, who has begun to hallucinate a new religion.

As Sister E. and I prepared breakfast, I saw Charles standing on the backstoop, peering through the kitchen door. When he knew that I had seen him, he knocked heartily. On Sister E.'s face was a serene yet stupefied air. After I opened the door, Charles cursed the doctor before finally telling us that Hans was dead. Sister E. relieved me of the tray, and I followed him to the men's cabin where Este was trying to catch Lucas who was smearing mud over the floors as glass shards cracked under his knees. Mud had been thrown against the far wall and the blanket that covered Hans was already splattered.

The sergeant was muttering that he wasn't sleeping in there until they cleaned it up and got rid of that damned Dutchman. Este was holding the boy by his wrist as he squirmed to break loose. The women were standing in the yard, asking what had happened and Charles kicked the door closed with his able foot and shuffled over to grab the boy by his other arm. The boy's face was caked in mud and his clumped eyelashes weighed down his flickering lids.

I opened the door and led the boy onto the porch, telling Louise to get him washed up. Mud on the far wall was leaking down through the floorboards. A puddle had enclosed Han's cot and the other cots were pushed further away. I almost slipped when I reached down to uncover him. His eyes and mouth were still open, and his scabbed hands had coiled and turned stiff. I swiped at some flies that had already settled on his forehead and covered his face with the counterpane. When I went back out into the yard, the scene was almost too chaotic to revisit very intimately in these lines. Sister M. frantically went past me as Louise was attempting to lift the boy who was flailing in her arms and tearfully rehearsing all the expletives he had learned during his vagrant days. The doctor staggered in his nightshirt and overalls while the men mocked his hurried and disheveled appearance with whistling and nervous gestures, his clumsy untangling of all the instruments in his valise, his apparent temerity before the specter of a corpse, so accustomed to the languorous, contemplative pace of lizards that he was flustered by the mayhem that awaited him outside his door.

Sister M. emerged from the men's cabin and crossed herself as Sister E. passed out beans, tack, and tea to the men who all remained in the yard while the women were served in their cabin. Sister E. and I proceeded to wrap and bind Hans' corpse in his own linens, after which Charles helped us to load it on the stretcher and carry it to the chapel.

The doctor excused himself and retreated to the scullery, possibly to recount in his journal the irrational intrusion of mortality and grief into a morning reserved for specimen collecting, the weight of a corpse, the petrified limbs, the senselessness of all the mundane possessions belonging to the deceased: the mantelpiece clock, the brittle calendar with its illustrated advertisements for tonics and tobacco, the dusty leather shoes, the steel comb, and the shaving blade, which all sat in one corner of the cabin, painted in mud, and belonging to whomever risked possessing them.

Charles fashioned a casket by late afternoon. The doors to the chapel were unbarred and the patients gathered around the shrouded corpse. Once more the lack of a priest entailed a curt ceremony in which Sister E. read *De profundis* and Sister M. mumbled a verse from Lamentations. Soon the chapel began to reek of decay, and the doors were held open with two chairs wedged into mud. The wind poured through and shook the candleflames that encircled the corpse. When most of the flames had been smothered, the sergeant wheeled along the edge of the wall and Ratherne scraped his cane until he arrived in the yard and lit his pipe.

One could perhaps attribute the suppressed sentiment of mourning among them to a number of impulses circulating the camp, the most prominent being the decreased significance of death for those who have been robbed of their homes and families and names. Because of the particular impediments due to the affliction, Hans was almost entirely unable to speak and the weakness of his body was such that he rarely raised upright. He relied on us to change his bedclothes and linens, and he had lately relied on the doctor to attend to his infected esophagus. But dwelling on these particulars does not account for the gift Hans imparted to his cabinmates. He listened with patience and reserve to what was confided in him and occasionally would struggle to utter cryptic strings of words in reply. Because of this, he was entrusted with the other men's words and became not unlike a confessor. Since speaking took such effort for him, the others could be assured he would never repeat their confessions and the few lucid words he was able to muster in response were imputed by those confessing with an oracular weight. This designation of Hans was partly the result of not having a resident priest, but I also believe even with a priest, the others would have still confided in Hans. Unlike a priest, Hans would not classify certain confessions as sinful, nor would he expect atonement for even the most heinous acts. For although a priest's face is concealed during confession, his voice may resound with judgment, and the ritual of the confession may render any harmless whim as a severe affront. The priest seeks not to unburden one of guilt, but to amplify its aspect, situating guilt and the sin that nurses it at the forefront of daily concern. Hans would merely listen to others, perhaps attempt to reply, and most likely forget whatever was said to him.

I sometimes wondered what Sister E. would say to Hans, if she said anything at all, during the hours in which she lingered over him. Did she pour forth reminiscences of her youth in Ontario, her marriage at the age of fourteen to a timber foreman, or had all those memories been overtaken by an imagined prehistory? Maybe she gossiped about who took a double share of stew for lunch, or what nicknames she had for which cats, or what clumsy trifle Sister M. had performed in the morning, or perhaps she speculated over what compelled me to bed before her and Sister M., what sullied spirit was I conjuring in my cell, what voice was I beseeching to plumb through me while I tossed and seized atop the springs?

If Hans were to have lived longer, all those spurious confessions and partly imagined memories would still be inaccessible. No history was lost that was not already unrepeatable for the one entrusted with the past was appointed as such precisely because utterance so often failed him. Without a confessor, the afflicted would either withhold their thoughts and risk the pangs of a bloated conscience, or divulge themselves to the other patients who may repeat what was said, or otherwise abuse the trust accorded them. Perhaps both Hans and the priest were suicides of residual sin, tortured by the visions unburdened to them. And without both of them to listen and deliver their judgment, the patients would confide their obsessions to us.

Sisters, however, should not be conferred with this authority. We listen, but are forever hesitant to respond. When asked how the Lord shall weigh some illicit thought or youthful betrayal, we stutter foolishly about the forgiving hand of God, wipe their brows with a soiled handkerchief, spill our beads into their grip and tell them all is redeemed when the soul is made empty for His loving grace.

Before I returned to the house, Sister M. tasked me with barring the chapel doors. This superfluous measure was not intended to safeguard the dead so much as preserve the sacredness of the structure for the doors were always barred unless the floor was in use. While I was locking the chain, Louise approached me, dragging the boy behind her. She demanded him to tell me why he slung mud in the men's cabin. I told her I was not troubled by a child's inclination. Louise shook the boy's arm. I removed the board and opened the doors, beckoning them out of the wind.

Why were you having a fit in the morning, Lucas, was it because you found Hans wasn't breathing, I asked. Because he wouldn't answer you when you woke up in the morning?

His blinking was erratic and he squinted through the lantern light that shone on his encrusted lids. Last night Hans was thirsty, he said, he was thirsty, and he told me to get a jar from the doctor's room. He frantically looked around the floor and walls as if looking for ways to escape. Louise tightened her hold on his arm, and the boy said he did what he was told. He said he missed Hans, and he wanted to hide him under all the mud so he wouldn't have to smell him anymore.

Louise took the boy back to the men's cabin. Before I barred the doors, I looked at the casket placed beneath the pulpit and considered the Church's forbiddance of proper burial for suicides, the absence of ceremony, the disposal in a potter's field or waste heap, the condemnation to purgatory, and I questioned the doctrinal validity of deeming suicide given another person was responsible for the actual administration of the lethal liquid which must have been obtained from the doctor's shelves. Death by such means was referred to in the camp as taking the Jew wine. The derivation of this particular colloquialism confounds me if it were equating the Semites with cowardice because anyone familiar with the character of Abraham would regard such an equation as absurd.

Hans had been enfeebled and bound to his cot for two years, and he surely understood the near certainty of never rising to walk again. He must have hidden the jar beneath his counterpane after the boy had stolen it. When the others had fallen asleep, he probably signaled the boy to pour the substance into his throathole. Although the epidermis of Hans was almost completely insensate, I imagine his organs must have burned as the liquid trickled through, and since the others did not awaken, he must have died quietly, inciting the boy to wander into the yard, kneel down and claw in the mud. Perhaps he wished to draft a note, if not a sober farewell, at least some cryptic addendum to his life, but he was physically unable to write and the boy was illiterate.

The Mother said that Hans had arrived with the nameless boy who preceded Lucas. The one who was apprehended in the street after repeated escapes from an orphanage and who arrived during winter of the second year with a bundle bound by twine to his back. Before he was renamed, he bedded beside the oven, warming his hands at the oven while the rest of the cabin slept. Because his fingers had been numbed by affliction, he failed to sense heat. His shivering drew him closer and his hand nestled among the coals. The others awoke to the stench and pulled the smoking hand from the oven. Some days after he was bandaged, rot had spread up his arm. The Mother awaited the arrival of a doctor so the arm could be severed, but a fever killed him before a doctor arrived, and he was buried without a name. His was the first stone to be set on the rise.

While feeding him one evening, I asked Hans if he remembered the boy's name, the one he rode with on an upriver coal barge, but he did not. He remembered traveling with a child and another man who was dressed in a suit and whose hand was wrapped in gauze. He remembered riding all night under a canvas tent, the boy crouched near the anchor rigging with his head wedged between his knees and rubbing his thighs for warmth, the pilot occasionally emerging on deck to sound the shoals.

Men on horseback were waiting on the riverbank, he said, and the barge had drifted along the bend before we were led through the gates where the sisters had set lamps on the path leading to the house. I told him that the boy was buried without a name, and he said the boy wasn't in camp but for a month. He remembered the boy sitting around and watching the men play cards, or disappearing after breakfast to go chase toads through the swamp.

Although Hans would claim to know more about the shifting patches of rot in the rafters than he did about his cabinmates, his recollections were surprising in their vastness and acuity. Perhaps he had also remembered all those confessions bestowed upon him, and if he were able to, he could have transcribed them into mock testimonies with melodramatic interludes, each entitled after its proprietary and unburdening soul, bound by ribbon, and stashed beneath the floorboards in a suitcase, but such archival fantasies need to be extinguished. All I can transcribe remains tethered to my own perilous eye, wherein resides all memories yet made salvageable.

At dusk the casket was lowered. After prayer we began filling up the pit so we could return to the house before nightfall. I said nothing to our de facto Mother about how Hans had died, partly to ensure he had a pedestrian burial but also because the nature of his death would most probably alarm her and result in manic reproaches towards the boy, the other men in the cabin, and myself. She told us to feed the patients just before burial, as if she intended to distract them from the camp's lascivious entanglement with death, that most dulcet of suitors, most learned in the carnal arts, purveyor of irresistible seduction, who allows but for the briefest respite before recommencing his ravishment. For her, repeatedly bearing witness to this orgy would lead to an incurable listlessness, which is much more debilitating than the affliction itself, as if a body were not truly afflicted until its soul were bereft of hope. She was not as worried about a patient's ailing condition as she was about the added labor of attending to both a diseased body and faithless spirit. She understood that the rigors of melancholia were much more irremediable than fractured bones or bronchitis or dysentery.

After the last shovelful of dirt, we marked the plot with a nameless stone and walked back to the house. The other two sisters hurried against the wind as if burial had awakened their appetite, and the doctor lingered past me, his hands resting in his vest pockets so he resembled a ruminative baron sauntering across his wintry manor.

I thought your creed didn't reserve customs like that for unnatural deaths, he said, standing at the back stoop with his hands still nestled upon his gut, enamored with his own stately posture, his fresh pale whiskers, studying the sky as if to deduce from the cloud's passage how much moisture the night would expunge and how slowly the mist would rise at first light and whether the wind would ever slacken. He said he sympathized with my discretion and to dishonor one death would dishonor the collective destiny of the patients. For what are they expected to achieve, he asked without seeming to address me, but to die with dignity?

Later that evening I wondered whether the listlessness, which Sister M. feared would beset the patients, had not already inhabited the doctor. Perhaps it accounted for his cynicism, surely heightened for my amusement, but unwarranted considering his recent arrival and the fact that before working at camp he was teaching reptilian anatomy to university students.

I could not sleep because of the shaking. In the past, when I reached the brink of fever and had to uncoil myself from my linens, the shaking was induced by the uneasy shift of season rather than any feminine malaise. However, since residing at the camp, where the seasons change gradually, I could account for no explanation other than a bland diet and the cumulative effects of fatigue.

I sat up to grip the bedposts and fastened my eyes, thinking of Hans' description of his journey upriver huddled among coal crates beside the nameless boy and the other arrival, each of them bracing themselves as the barge veered through sharp passages to the pounding of the engine. My own journey upriver left me imagining the faint sounds of night that the engine overwhelmed, the barge creaking over unsteady waters, a sound not unlike the walls of my cell hardening in winter when the splinters protrude from the pitch lathered between the boards. Against the roar, I heard the overhanging cypress limbs rustling with possum, the water threshing as shoals were sounded. Drifting across the wide straights, where the stars glowed through the shredded canvas and billowing steam, the gust whistled with a bite, burning through fabric and lashing at my face.

I saw the tide as so many fingers sprawling over the barge, pouring over the passengers before it lifted their frantic bodies while the tugboat collapsed, trapping the pilot inside his sinking cabin, leaving the unmanned barge to turn course downriver, followed by those who shall not drown but drift through viscous folds until they tangle in the reeds. The barge hovered through hushed channels, and my numb hands settled at my sides, relinquished of any desire to fend off the overflowing tide.

When Paul was brought to the front door in shackles, he stood beside a deputy, shivering and naked in what looked like a woman's bathrobe. He seemed neither distraught nor abashed by his forced return to the camp. The ravages of his tongue had apparently spread to his lips and chin, so that his entire face seemed to collapse into his mouth, which was wrought as one perforated pustule that he could barely move when the deputy asked him whether he would stay put this time.

Go home, otherwise you might catch what I got, he said, his lips peeled back from his slurred words. While unlocking the shackles, the deputy said, If I'm going to catch it, I already have.

He stepped onto the pathway and told Paul he didn't want to find him in the city again before briskly tipping his hat to Sister M. and myself as if to enact atonement before turning toward the river.

We led Paul around the side of the house, across the yard, and into the men's cabin where they barely grumbled at the sight of Paul returning, as if they knew his freedom were shortlived. The captured patient walked across the cabin and sat down in the empty cot that had belonged to Hans. He did not inquire about the fate of his former cabinmate. The empty cot dispelled all speculation.

The canvas stretched over the windowframe was rippling in the wind. He rubbed his sore wrists and unlaced his boots and was still sitting on the edge of the cot when Sister M. and I returned to the house to prepare breakfast.

She told me to place Paul's release form in the top lefthand drawer of the parlor desk. This chaotic drawer was reserved for miscellany documents and receipts. Both Sister M. and the deputy had signed the form where it stated which parties held custody over the transported patient. According to the form, the patient was legally bound to the camp and to the care of Sister M. At the bottom of the page, beside the date, was a line reserved for Paul's signature, but since he was unable to write his name, his shivering hand marked the line:

XXXX

When we returned to the men's cabin with breakfast, Paul had changed into the trousers and jacket he had left behind. The other men were served on the table beside the door while Paul took his tray and sat back down on his cot, accusing the others of stealing his other clothes and hiding them under their cots.

It's your fault for leaving them behind, Charles said, scooping up more porridge. We don't ask you to give back what you took from us.

Paul sat up in his cot the rest of the morning, nodding off with his hands buried in his trouser pockets, flecks of stewed carrots and onions smeared over his abscesses. With drooping lids, he cursed the others for taking his things. His head swayed as if he were still chugging upriver with the deputy whistling across deck. He pulled his frayed gown tighter, clenching his jaw as if the noxious plumes stung his mouth. Pus trickled down his chin. He was unable to sleep, yet undone by the most implacable weariness.

He had tried and failed to escape on three occasions. The first two attempts failed because he had decided to house with his brother, who forever cowed to his stentorian wife and relayed his whereabouts to the police. His latest attempt probably failed in a similar fashion, which must have accounted partly for his vociferous curses and belligerence.

When the doctor arrived to retrieve him, he easily complied and shuffled across the cabin and into the yard. The women were sitting on their porch, and the boy was cartwheeling across the walkway slats to the victrola's screeching hymns. All of the women, save Cybele who was filing Ratherne's fingernails, watched him as he crossed to the scullery, his head down and hands clasped together, as if he still believed himself to be in shackles, until he unexpectedly lifted his head and turned toward the grandmother.

You wrangle the best chicken, he said, I'll carve it up tonight. He uttered his words loud enough that he was heard despite his slurred stammering.

The grandmother did not tell him that all the fowl had been killed off, mostly by the roaming cats who had lately began sleeping in the barn with the lone cow, an aging matriarch nearly dry and kept alive more out of sympathy than any distinct usefulness. When the cats first housed in the barn, the cow was groaning nervously and charging the walls with its frail head, but it had soon become accustomed to the itinerant presence of the cats, even their bloodthirsty spats failed to rouse her from sleep. When the barndoors were unlatched, the cats were slumbering in the hay, deferring to the queen as she sauntered out for her morning graze, some rolling in the dust and strands, one with its tail sinuously sketching the light while the rest of its body was buried in the shade.

In the scullery, I transcribed the doctor's observations, worrying whether my hand would be fit later on for an evening stroll across the page. He described the bruises and lacerations on Paul's body and wondered whether they were all attributable to the affliction. His jaw, which at first I assumed to be infected, could have easily been bloodied by repeated kicks and punches. When the doctor questioned him about his injuries, he said his mouth used to feel numb inside, but now it burned and sometimes he wanted to cut his lips off and uproot his tongue.

The rest of the day Paul would continue to curse the other men for stealing his clothes and Hans for bequeathing his stench to the cabin. We were absent from his curses, not because he believed we would unburden him of his own curse, but rather because, within his nearly ungraspable past, there resided recollections of a smoky aisle resounding with a voice which he was forced to listen or otherwise bear the switch thirtyfold and be forbidden from play the following week. He had learned like many other patients to regard with reverence the slow gestures that seemed to seduce his elders, the morning light parsed and distilled over the robes cascading through the aisles, those slender fingers lowering a cracker upon his tongue, the lifting of the cup to that same frail light.

As a child, all of this must be heeded for when the others echoed a word or gesture, so must he, or else risk being dragged out to the street by his ear alongside the crowd solemnly returning home. Soon his involvement in the rituals enacted under that murky, narrow ceiling would become instinctual, and although the course of his thoughts would often wander elsewhere, he would still appear fully observant to his elders, echoing each word with conviction, appearing both jubilant and serene during communion. If he ever succumbed to cursing God like Job, he would have done so beyond earshot of our coven while his cabinmates scraped tobacco across the table, or perhaps they joined him in his invective against a holy upbringing until the cabin resounded with chants of apostasy.

But given their familiar quarters and isolation from the outer world, if blame was to be dealt, it was dealt among them, not unlike a pack of cats fighting over a bird that squirms in the dirt, each aware of the last scraps of dignity which cannot be evenly apportioned, the most ruthless gorge with frenzied delight while the timid clasp their guts in agony. And yet to offset this battle for diminished dignity, the patients were intrinsically bound by an empathic force, namely, their shared condition. Without it, they were strangers mandated to live as one family, prisoners without guards or walls, sentences or reprieves, and yet if they escaped and were caught, they would be promptly returned.

While prisoners have an authority to rail against, the patients had but each other upon whom to vent the pangs of their confinement. If I were to step in and bear a splinter of their wrath, I would retreat to my cell afterward, seeking a modicum of composure.

Sister M. may have remarked on my Irish fortitude, how I performed each task with almost mechanical callousness, but if a patient were to accost me, or damn their fate in the breath of my creed, I would wander into the river like the Mother in her fever throes, turning back to face the house before submerging my head. The camp, however, was no place for such histrionics. One learns to ingest all penumbra, or else become ensconced in darkness.

After the doctor had treated Paul's wounds and the hapless escapee was snoring atop the table, he told me to transcribe the name and dosage of a medicine procured from his shelf. The label bore a Latin name, which I failed to recognize, my knowledge of the language mostly being relegated to doctrinal concerns. The liquid looked clear with perhaps a slight brownish hue that permeated the glass in a thin cloud. For a liquid to have such a color, it must have been extracted from vegetal matter.

While the doctor was scrubbing his hands in the basin, I uncorked the vial. The liquid was odorless, the scent of ink scrawled on the label smelled stronger. It was unusually viscous and no reaction seemed to occur when I shook the vial.

I puzzled over whether to ask the doctor about the medicine's origin and purpose, but I feared such rampant curiosity could unnerve him, as if I doubted his measures, and was forever casting him as some crank academic, unsuited for these disastrous climes for his neck still bore the fat of the city, but lately he had seized his back when bending over a patient and his legs were bandaged from all the bites he had accumulated. Soon, I feared, we would need to carry him by wheelbarrow into town while people rose from their rocking chairs to corral their children indoors.

The doctor said he wished to see Paul the same time tomorrow while the patient took his leather hat from the peg beside the door, where the doctor hung his canvas sack for lizard collecting, his own hat and scarf, and his satchel of instruments. Paul's hat was so stiffened that it threatened to slide from his nearly hairless scalp.

To fit it more squarely, he had to fold the edges so the cracks already formed in the leather crumbled further, and liquid the color of ember dripped from the brim.

On the porch of the men's cabin, Paul asked why the doctor wanted to see him the following day. I did not tell him that he intended to treat him with a unknown medicine, partly to avoid having him tell his cabinmates about it, any mention of which could cause panic or unruly excitement. Since the doctor abstained from divulging its mystery to me, I assumed he wished to keep it a secret from the patients as well, evidently unaware of its actual effects beyond the results printed in medical journals.

That evening I considered telling Sister M. that the doctor was intent on experimenting with a new medicine, but I knew she would discover it on her own soon enough, just as she would one day overhear mention of the suicide which occurred under her leadership, or the runes which stained the newly turned earth of the pecan grove. The more Sister M. believed she was privy to, while in actuality knowing very little, the more orderly the camp would be. It was better for all of us if she remained in the parlor divan with her tabby nestled by her side, reading the month old city newspaper, and enshrouded in her own eminence.

I awoke before the rest of the camp and heard sanguine voices from other sealed chambers as if my delirium avowed to keep me company. My footsteps down the staircase clinked like the ceremonious chiming of crystal, or like the banister had shed icicles to the floor. From the hallway, I heard the backdoor open and swiftly went downstairs into the kitchen, but the door was firmly latched. In the parlor mirror, I saw my hair uncovered and tangled and beneath my eyes hung gruesome furrows flaked with sleep. Out in the yard a straggling pair of cats slid among the weeds with loping eyes cast afar, punished by the remainder of the pack and scavenging for refuse, expected to return to the barn with their bounty laid in the middle of the encircling pack, a token of penance soon consumed by all.

I returned to my chamber to retrieve my cornice and went back downstairs to the kitchen. As I filled the oven, I saw Paul perched on the steps of the woman's cabin, cloaked in his bathrobe, enacting his drowsy vigilance over the cabin, or awaiting one of the women to emerge. I leaned closer to the window where he may have seen me for his eyes seemed aligned with the kitchen door and his mouth contorted into a painful grin, or else he was again soothing his wounds with his tongue and sucking at the pus. I stepped back and stoked the coals forcefully as the pot began to boil, cloaking the window.

He had departed when I went out to the yard to gather more kindling. From the rise I could smoke spreading across the sky. Pine needles and pools were agleam, and the night chill was unrelenting. Atop the levee herons stalked, patiently scoping the depths, birds of such shrewd intelligence one is forever tempted

61

to impute the qualities of man upon them, possessed of singular intent, attached to a stretch of land solely for what may be reaped thereof, and if hunger or danger ever flusters them, they soon aspire to poise, or flap their wings to conceal their shame.

In the late morning, the doctor distilled the unknown medicine in a bowl with a tincture and administered it to him. After swallowing it with some strain, Paul sat on the table as if awaiting further treatment, never asking during the simple procedure why he was chosen to drink the liquid or what symptoms it was indeed intended to alleviate. Perhaps its effects were unseen and the bacterium itself was supposed to evaporate, leaving buoyant cells to prosper unimpeded. The doctor examined the patient's eyes and lifted his jaw to inspect the roof of his mouth by lamplight before excusing him from the scullery.

The doctor wrote about the acceleration of decay that had beset the patient, the stupor that commanded his bearing, how he reeled into frenetic, nonsensical speech, the appearance of bruises which seemed as if they formed the day before when in fact they had not healed for days. He puzzled in the margins upon Paul's avowed sensations of pain, not solely in those areas where he was injured but in the afflicted portions as well, finally speculating upon whether 'pain stimuli were symptomatic of the disease's diminishment,' suggesting again that the affliction may render one numb to stimuli. Sifting through his notes, I dreaded the likelihood of being asked to structure his scattered fragments into coherent prose, so that, when he returned to the city, he could convince his superiors he persevered with his research despite his perilous residence, and they could in turn honor him with a ceremony and assign him a more privileged position, one which did not necessitate interacting with patients.

After bundling the pages into a stack and tying them, I washed mud from the examination table. Under the lamplight, it bore faint scratches and swathes of exposed shavings still glistening with water.

The doctor lowered his hand into one of the bowls on the shelf. When he pulled it out, a newly captured lizard had enwrapped its tail around his finger. The doctor lifted the lizard, a gesture that pacified the creature, even causing it to slightly recoil its limbs and tuck its head into the folds of its neck. As the tail began slipping from his finger, the pliant tip danced along his flesh, sensing the curve of his finger and gripping it more securely. He dangled the lizard before his face, watching its fragile head writhe with closed lids, gingerly tasting the air.

Are you familiar, Sister, with the process of autotomy, he asked. Without deducing the etymology, I answered that I was not.

This lizard will sever itself from its own tail, he said, lowering the creature back inside the bowl, after which it scurried upward towards the opening before retreating to the bottom as he fastened the lid. He said he had read accounts of the tail snapping and twisting for minutes after severance, which surprised the predator and allowed the lizard to escape.

This severing is by no means a painless process, he said, the tail may take months to regrow, a significant percentage of any lizards' lifetime, especially without an appendage that's vital to its equilibrium, but the lizard will risk this to survive the momentary threat of death.

He walked over to the desk and shook his tin cup to unsettle the coffee grounds while I stood in the doorway to await his permission to leave. The anole did not sever its tail while in the doctor's grip, as if it knew he were a harmless admirer who preferred starches and grains and beasts of a larger order. After he dropped into the bowl, it rested its belly at the bottom as the other lizards clung to the side, nervously extending their tongues.

He clinked his tin cup in a flurry with his scalpel and walked over to his bed. He unlaced and removed his shoes and set the cup beside his swollen foot. Please excuse my question, Sister, if it may seem insolent, but do you believe that the faithless have a chance to be healed?

I hesitated to answer, shifting closer to the door which had stopped shuddering, letting the crisp gleam part the room, flicker among the bowls and steel contrivances, the stained splits of tablewood.

I have seen the faithless fully recover from their illness, I said, and I have seen the most devout tortuously succumbing to death over many months.

Through the crack in the door, the yard was dim, and the weeds were flattened into a pale tapestry. Kindling in the fireplace rustled and ash sucked upward into a cloud. The last strands of hair smeared to his scalp tumbled across his forehead as he nodded feebly, reaching for the blanket folded at the foot of his bed and wrapping it around his shoulders.

He was so beset by fever he wished to discuss theological matters half an hour before the lunch bell, but his constitution would not allow it. Before closing his eyes, he asked me to stir the embers. The lizards pattered across their bowls, stirred into flight by the sight of a moth circling the lamp.

The morning chill stung my legs as I crossed the floor, slipped on my habit, and awaited the quietness of the house to stir for it never muffled the echoes which assailed it. Our harried grumbling, ovengrates howling with frost. On my knees at the foot of the bed, my prayer exhaled in steam. I saw the house crumbling into shards the color of iron, hyacinth draped in insidious dew, the splendor of the river's thaw, cackling herons with violent smattering feathers, patients returning to earth who may finally open their eyes and wish to remain awake, attuned to the warbler's reveille, vast walls of oaks slackened and shedding mist, followed by muskrat who retreated with scarce bounty into their hovels of rot.

The banister was too cold to touch, so I put my hands into my vestment. Dust that had resisted all sweeping was wedged into the coarsened mantel, the panels of the corridor, beneath the glass of the general's daguerreotype, clouding his pristine suit and trimmed whiskers, the eyes of the hound posed upright beside him. The polished floor was imprinted with paws prints looping in and out of the kitchen, scattered with meal and crockery.

I gathered the meal into a cup and poured all of it into one of the sacks not yet riddled by claws. Before the window was covered by steam, I saw a band of squirrels combing the weeds, barking at one another across the yard where Paul was curled up in his bathrobe, his face burrowed in leaves. I wiped the glass again with my sleeve and stared at the doctor's appointed test subject as if to confirm whether he were a lapsed specter of prayer, or the frozen heap of a man coiled like a mollusk beneath shed oak limbs and a frostbit glow.

I set the ladle on its hook and untied my apron before heading into the yard, the squirrels rallying to their heights at first whisper of my vestment, first sight of this bloated raven frantically brandishing its wings as it touched earth.

I leaned over him and repeated his name. He was not shivering and his pulse was steady. His fingers were their usual shade of blue while the blood from his tongue had congealed on his chin as if he had been chewing on it throughout the night. I rolled him over on his back to discover a flattened pile of excrement, his bathrobe stained with vomit.

Nudging his shoulder caused his eyes to finally open and the shivering to commence. To the sound of his name he signaled no acknowledgement and braced his gut, gagging as strings of blood dripped among the weeds. I held him beneath his arms to help him to his feet while he said his mouth burned, and he didn't want to go inside the cabin. He dragged his feet in the mud, as if he were an ailing wolf that had abandoned its pack and sought to spare them the spectacle of its death, or perhaps, as the more cynical commentators of nature would have it, the wolf prefers the anonymity of scavengers to the prospect of being devoured by its own pack.

Once we were inside the cabin, I led him to his cot where he slipped from his soiled gown and curled up, shivering in his blankets. Before the wind swung open the door and whistled through the oven, the other men were all waking up save the boy whom I nearly stepped on when walking over to stir the embers.

He smells worse than Hans did, the sergeant said, sitting up in his cot. His legs were twitching under his blanket, recurrent spasms he himself could but witness with slumbering curiosity, but which never failed to entrance him, and on occasion he had been known to entertain his cabinmates with the balletic contortions of his toes, a phenomenon which coincidently happened in the evening after the gambling stakes had been depleted and the women had left the yard.

As I returned with breakfast, I saw the men on the porch through the wafting steam from the porridge, watching me without their usual famished fixation. I climbed up the steps with trays balanced on either arm, and they wearily took their bowls when I passed them out.

I entered the cabin and stood before Paul's cot where black spools stained the mattress and dripped to the floor. Those clumps that had clung to him had melted and smeared beneath him as he twisted with his arms wrapped around his gut.

When the doctor arrived, he crossed the cabin with annoyance, as if he had not drunk his precious coffee that morning. He tucked his shirttail into his trousers and tried to open Paul's eyes, but his lids were clamped tightly and eking out tears that stuck to his lashes. The doctor said that such a reaction to the medicine was not unexpected and even desirable, considering how benign his fever was.

The boy had arisen from the floor, tugging at my tunic. I led him outside where he sat with the bowl and fed himself with his cupped palm. I did not know whether such behavior was due to his vagrant upbringing, or because his diminished vision induced a helpless disposition, which I attempted to counteract by conferring responsibilities upon him, such as conveying dirty utensils to the kitchen, fetching water and dressing supplies or helping the grandmother gather vegetables.

The doctor said when Paul warmed up, he should bathe and eat, and he himself would return to administer a second dose. I sat by the patient's bedside while his shivering became less severe. The men could not withstand the stench and lingered on the porch as the grandmother made her rounds to the pump, lugging the bucket across the yard, seemingly gaining fortitude with each journey.

Paul ceased cursing the other patients and instead questioned me about his whereabouts. The more I answered him, the more his memory steadily expanded in depth, and yet he insisted he could not return to camp. He believed himself to be elsewhere, the city perhaps, or another outpost along the river, attended to by a nun who claimed to recognize him and who reminded him of where he was from, why he was there, the names of the men speaking on the porch, why their voices seemed so frail.

He remembered awaking in the yard, feeling terribly ill, unable to move, and yet he failed to recollect why he had left the cabin in the middle of the night, or when he began feeling ill. Sister E. made her rounds to the pump and we boiled water and poured it into the basin and left him alone to bathe in the cabin.

The mist became more translucent as it lifted and brushed against the house. Ratherne had returned to the third cabin to cover the windows. I walked across camp to awaken the cow from its stubborn sleep induced by gorging. After leading her into the barn, I stepped inside the dairy room piled with clumps of hay. According to the Mother, a patient was bound by rope in the dairy room while awaiting transport to the courthouse upriver for murdering another patient. She never revealed his motive to us and we must have been too enthralled by her story to ask.

From what she told us, I assumed the murder resulted from two men squabbling in their cabin over some trifle probably involving a female patient. The victim's head was pummeled upon a stove and his body discarded into the swampland. Although all evidence was lost save for drops of blood inside the men's cabin, the murderer confessed and was locked up in the barn according to the inaugural priest's orders.

For nearly two weeks, the murderer barely budged from his corner, declined all but water and tack and would tell no one where he disposed of the body. The Mother said that because of his disfigured feet and hands, he could have perhaps escaped his bindings, and when the convoy arrived and properly shackled him, he left peaceably, even crossing himself before the priest.

We asked the Mother if any witnesses among the patients were brought to court when he was tried, but she said his trial never occurred due to lack of evidence, and she received word that he would be shipped back, but he never was, which was probably for the better since his return would have caused alarm and possible retaliation from the patients. The Mother also said that the cow had become quite obsequious to the murderer's cues, tossing in its girdle when he shuffled his feet and stomping to his whistles. This last flourish was most likely accentuated by the Mother to end her account with some jest after describing how the sisters and the priest set out morning after morning in various directions, wading through brush to find the victim, a wizened patient who suffered seizures and played the fiddle after supper, but after each search they returned without a body and eventually burned his lousy garments beneath the levee and stored his fiddle in the house.

Having washed the bowls and utensils after lunch and ensuring the line was stripped of linen and the next batch was scrubbed in the basin, the river being too cold for stepping in, I was grateful for an hour's rest in my chamber, too exhausted to write yet too restless for slumber while my voice was much too hoarse for prayer, having strained itself through the dispelling of Paul's morning amnesia.

A gnat cleaned itself on my pillow, almost disintegrating

before the whiteness, its wings angling in the slightest drafts beneath the door. I sat at the foot of the bed, yearning for the monotony of a window, even a hatch facing the sky, or a circular pane fixed beneath the ceiling and fastened by a rusted latch. I would risk whatever cold seeped through glass to watch leaves crash and clouds plunge headlong into those pale wasted canerows.

The gnat was tangled in the cross stitch, its yellow wings draped over its legs. When I spun those threads back North, I would lean into the mule, searching for a break in the stitch, the narrowest sliver through which the murky factory gleam would part, but the cross stitch would withstand the light. Flies that usually hovered in the heights sometimes sifted closer to the floor, lured by the sweet dampness of our wrists and armpits. After tasting our flesh, some of them would stick to the fabric, staggering across the threaded pitfalls, their bulbous eyes flitting beneath tiny hairs.

Slipping into the house through a crack in a windowpane, or a door briefly opened downstairs, the creature must have strayed into my chamber and circled the ceiling for a means of escape, but I had latched the door behind me after I entered, thus trapping the gnat, which probably fell to the pillow in exhausted defeat. When it landed on my pillow, it discovered that it was not solely confined to this room, but now trapped by the cross stitch.

I prayed silently and could not sleep. I had visions of a village stormed by an infectious curse, mules of a factory floor igniting in flames, spinsters trapped by smoke, journeymen gathered on riverbanks, seized by rattling tongues, mangled recitations of the last book, all awaiting to be quenched by a fount of bourbon poured by a penniless preacher who awaits his own benediction by kneeling in the waters, held under by his followers until the devil beckons him, and he is set adrift, soon to reemerge downriver, arms held aloft, both his disdain for his drunken followers and his facility to proselytize reinvigorated, a novitiate to the destiny of mud.

Unable to close my eyes, my hands trembled. After a bout of feverish prayer, a window would be but petty consolation. I could hear the gnat's wings flitting, a hushed squeal cruelly attesting to its failure at flight. I imagined the doctor grabbing the creature by its wings, lowering it into the bowl for the lizard's tongue to seize, or perhaps the gnat would be fortunate enough to fly from the bowl before the lizard could devour it, escaping the scullery only to arrive on my pillow, already falling from fortune to misfortune in its brief life, awaiting salvation through death, or the grace of happenstance, but no wind passed through my chamber, and the gnat further bound itself by flitting its wings.

I could have rescued the creature, albeit not one of the more blessed ones, yet integral to the survival of other creatures since its timeless inception. I lifted it by its wings, careful not to crush its body, and watched the undulations of its eyes, the gentle gnawing motion of its mouth. How long before the lizard would unfurl its tongue, lavish the gnat with its hungry gaze, appreciating the contours of its prey as if a more patient understanding of what it was about to devour would further satiate its appetite, infusing its digestive repose with more satisfaction, as if it were envisioning the gnat slowly decomposing within its stomach, the limbs leaking into its bones, the head crushed and coursing through its veins.

I imagined how the lizard's eyes would dilate as acidic saliva dripped across its tongue, how its toes would flinch while the gnat threw itself against the glass, beating itself mercilessly until assuming weary flight just above the hunter's upturned head. But the capture is fulfilled almost invisibly, the hunter motionless save for a meager lump passing beneath its taut flesh.

I held my breath and closed my eyes. One hand in my lap, the other rigidly composed, gripping the gnat by its wings. If I were to swallow the creature, how rapidly would the venomous swill of my stomach disintegrate it before it churned through my organs? I heard footsteps down the hall and opened my eyes. The sight of the shriveled creature dangling by its wings was enough to cure my unnatural appetite.

I wandered the empty rooms, sweeping floors and scraping mold from the walls with a butterknife. Some of the rooms had windows that were coated in dust, some had floors with holes that permitted one to look down upon other empty rooms where flecks of the rotten floor had drifted and scattered. Some rooms provided storage for broken chairs and table parts and disused cots. All the rooms were always locked save for a small maidchamber downstairs behind the scullery that had no lock on its door. The room was empty according to Sister M.'s stipulation, borne of fear that any unprotected item in the household could be stolen. The mold on the walls was of a brackish hue and stained the wallpaper peeling along the corners. I pulled back the curtains of the baywindow. The canopy sprawling westward shimmered with dull green light as dusk cloaked the river in a single gesture, soothing the flow that would increase its speed at nightfall.

The room beside the Mother's bedchamber stored ledgers and an inventory of shells and stones she had dug from the mud and kept in a wooden jewelry box. I imagined Sister M. slipping into the room at night, so soundless even her tabby remained asleep, touching the ribbed bright interior of the shells, polishing them with the hem of her nightshirt, pressing the coldness of the stones to her cheek in the summer months, recalling the Mother's sermons, the most memorable of which for me was when she spoke of the two orders of suffering that confront the soul. The first order entails that one is fully aware of their suffering and its degenerative onslaught, and that memories of a time in which the pain was minimal seem deceptive, even torturously so in that they intensify one's awareness of the deluge. The second occurs to those who are unaware that they suffer and yet still inhabit a world ransacked of wonders both glorious and inglorious.

As she spoke, I remembered many of the patients stared at the floor and appeared hungry and spiritless. The boy Lucas was slouched over, his body twitching with reverie while Sister E. stood beside the altar, ready to intone the designated psalm. The patients considered themselves to be of the first order, even if many were numb to physical pain. Once more, an emissary of the divine was telling them that their awareness of suffering afforded them a purer vision of the cosmos.

Of all the sermons I heard the Mother give, she never pretended that those who suffered were among the elect. According to her, all of us are aware of our own suffering. Awareness therefore is not the catalyst for salvation, resignation is. Suffering marks the advent of the soul, not its apotheosis. Charles asked her if resignation meant not showing your pain to others, and the Mother replied that pain demands to be expressed and to conceal it is akin to smothering the soul.

When I arrived at the men's cabin, Sister E. told me she had found Paul balled up on the backstoop, shivering in his gown. We urged him to drink tea while he sat up in his cot, his torn gown stained with vomit, shredded leaves and dirt stuck to his mouth. He would not swallow, and the tea spilled down his chin.

I told him it was to warm him up, but he insisted that I had soaked the tealeaves in the doctor's poison and boiled it for more strength. I sipped it to prove my honesty, but he still refused to drink it.

When the doctor arrived, he began raving with his back against the wall and pulled the sheet to his mouth, smearing it with bloody pus. The doctor told him his reaction to the medicine was to be expected and tried to force open his eyes, which darted across the ceiling after colliding with light. After tiring himself, he finally succumbed to the doctor's insistence and sipped the liquid for nearly a minute before coughing up a greenish froth and clasping his gut. The doctor asked me to retrieve the syringe from his valise, and I crossed the yard and greeted Ratherne who was sitting on the edge of his porch, lighting his pipe with a flaring woodchip that withstood the careening gusts. He watched me suspiciously as if I were retrieving more poison from the doctor's keep, a place he himself refused to visit regardless of the infection that persisted around his severed knee.

The fireplace was burning ferociously inside the scullery, and the glass bowls were sweating. Before he left, the doctor must have let loose his newly captured anole, which clung to the ceiling, or perhaps he let it loose before going to bed, allowing the lizard to better investigate its environs during its feeding hours, cleansing the scullery of mosquitoes that straggled in from the cold, or termites that nested in the floor, and yet what was most surprising about the anole was its obedience to the doctor as if he had trained it to patrol the scullery at night while it rested within its bowl during the day. The other lizards were pacified behind the sweating glass. It must have been that lizard alone which was permitted nocturnal freedom and soon it would be returned to its bowl, perhaps fed an ant husk before its lids closed and its skin drooped over its pulsing neck veins.

I pulled the valise from beneath the bed and dug through a myriad of instruments, untangling rubber tubes from prongs and wooden splints, almost piercing my thumb on the syringe before putting it in my pocket. On the table, pages were spread about, some with only a few words, some resembling engineering plans for primeval machines. Other sheets bore detailed drawings of salamanders, toads, dragonflies, and orchids, each specimen entitled under its Latin genus and glazed over with moist charcoal dust. When I returned to the cabin, the men had arisen and were shedding their bedclothes while the doctor fidgeted with his pocketwatch and Paul writhed atop his sheets. I held the tip of the syringe in boiling water and handed it to the doctor whose concentration shifted seamlessly from one instrument to another while the sergeant asked the doctor if the serum was supposed to make Paul crazy enough so he didn't rightly know how sick he was.

I rid Paul of his repulsive gown, carried it outside, stuffing it in a bucket and crossing the yard to the kitchen where I found the last phosphor sticks in a box behind the oven. Midway up the rise, I struck one of them and set the gown aflame, listening to the sound of the threads shrieking as the whole rotten heap was consumed, wafting with a horrendous stench that forced me to climb further up the rise, where the plume now passed before my line of sight.

Over the crackling flames I heard a woman's voice shouting down below. I stepped through smoke and saw the doctor clutching his arm, staggering in the yard while the grandmother called out for us. The doctor removed his jacket and touched his arm where blood had stained his torn shirt.

I picked the syringe up from the weeds and pocketed it as the doctor headed for the scullery, snapping the weeds with his frantic stride while the grandmother returned to the garden and Sister E. hurried back to the house. When I stepped inside the cabin, Charles was shaving above the basin and asked me why the doctor wouldn't give him any medicine.

Paul seemed to be asleep, or else was feigning sleep to avoid being scolded by the likes of Sister M. who was probably still cuddled beside her tabby under the netting she had draped across the bedframe. Beside Paul's cot sat the bowl of tincture that rippled as if a fly had just taken flight from its surface. I removed the syringe and set it across the bowl, noticing drops of blood speckled on the tip, the barrel nearly emptied of the fluid which was now pooling in the doctor's capillaries, sloshing around his organs, deceiving his weakened constitution into further malady, so that it perhaps mimicked symptoms of the affliction.

Lifting up the canvas flap from the window, I could see fire smoldering inside the steel bucket while Sister E. crossed the yard with a breakfast tray. She climbed the steps of the women's cabin, bowing her head at the threshold as if to summon the last vestiges of mercy before entering.

He kept telling the doctor that he didn't want that needle, the sergeant said. For a sick man, his aim's still good.

I dreaded Sister M. hearing of what had transpired, rushing to the men's cabin, and marching Paul to the washbasin where she would scrub his shivering body while the patients gathered on the men's porch.

I knocked on the scullery door, and the doctor bid me entrance. I sat both the bowl and the syringe on the table beside the scattered pages while he sat at his desk, cleaning his wound with a scrap of gauze.

He asked me if I could return in the afternoon and bring Este with me. He said he would not be taking breakfast and turned his chair toward the wall, dressing his arm while his back gleamed with sweat. The pile of paper shuffled as the anole emerged from beneath a sheet, trailing across the doctor's disparate notations before slithering behind a book.

Mud had hardened after two weeks without rain and a nocturnal mapping of crystal had left tendrils of frost outstretched down cypress limbs, its coolness melting through marrow and sap. Cybele was shaving Ratherne on the third cabin's porch while the girl and the grandmother turned layers of soil to thaw, reaping worms blinded by the afternoon radiance.

Este was napping on the porch when I awoke him and told him that the doctor had requested him. As Charles and I were lowering him into his wheelchair, the sergeant told him not to let the doctor give him any medicine. Pushing him on those rotten wheels into the scullery, I was admittedly awestruck by what the doctor had achieved since I had last taken notation at his desk.

He had transformed a disused washbasin into one of the primeval machines I had seen illustrated among the pages scattered on the table, which had been cleared away and fastidiously scrubbed. Neither the psychic wounds of humiliation nor the physical injury done to his left arm seemed to hinder his energy in the least, as if the fever that lately pestered him had been eradicated by the unexpected injection of medicine.

I sat down again and transcribed the procedure, beginning with the doctor lifting Este onto the table where he examined the reflexes of his legs. The doctor asked him how long he'd been unable to walk, and he told him when he first arrived at the camp, he was in bed for weeks with a fever. Finally, when he was well enough to get up, he slid from his cot and crumbled to the floor, gashing his head. He had been crippled ever since.

For the preliminary exam, I recorded how the patient's legs appeared to be insensate, rather unsurprising given their general

77

immobility, but what the doctor especially requested I transcribe was the physical condition of Este's legs, which seemed sturdy and without discoloration or rheumatism.

For the doctor, this indicated that the affliction had retreated from his legs and that perhaps the bacterium was thus more susceptible to treatment. After the doctor poured water into the basin, Este removed his shirt and trousers while still seated on the table, asking if it was going to hurt.

I don't want to end up like Paul, he said.

Water leapt from the basin, and the ceiling was enveloped in steam. The lizard bowls were streaked with drops. Este climbed into the basin without grimacing or closing his eyes. He calmly watched the doctor lift another basin atop the one he sat within, thereby almost completely enclosing him but for a portion cut into the top half which afforded a place for the steam to escape and a hole through which he could watch the doctor calibrating the heat by piling on more kindling from the fireplace

The doctor said that if bacterium infects the peripheral nerves, then sweat may cleanse the body, but the subject must be exposed to the highest temperature immediately, stunning the bacterium so it became less resistant and please notice, he continued, how the subject communicates no discomfort during treatment. Only when sensation returns to his body, he said, will the affliction begin to weaken to total dormancy.

He waited till the embers had cooled and steam had emptied through the scullery door before he stated the time, uncovered the basin, and asked me to help lift Este onto the table where I dried him and handed him his clothes. The hair on his legs was singed and his face was swollen. After he dressed, I gave him water, and he asked if he had to take the horseblood. The doctor told him it wasn't horseblood that he had given Paul.

If you took a drop of that stuff, he said, it would kill you.

Earlier that morning, Charles had spoken about horseblood with the sergeant while they sat on the porch, unable to enter the cabin because of Paul's stench. Such medicine had become synonymous with crank cures, and yet each patient also heard rumors of its curative force. The serum was administered like a tincture either through oral ingestion or epidermal injection and caused one to become horribly ill, as the body combated the infectious toxins. For those beset with the affliction, the serum too often proved lethal for their constitutions, and the silhouette of a horse and rider crossing the levee at dusk compelled many a patient to retreat to their cabin and cross themselves with oblations.

At the doctor's desk I tidied the notes and placed them in Este's file. On the bottom of the last page, I wrote a phrase from Ovid, Nec moderator adest, wondering if the doctor would recognize its origin. If he could not perceive folly in attempting to demystify the plague, then all his art would abandon him, and he would be undone by what he attempted to master, yet only after the river had been filled with the bloated corpses of those whom his art had failed to cure.

On the second Monday of each month, the post boy arrived with his satchel. Each time it seemed like a different boy from town was charged with the task, most likely paid a nickel to deliver the post, or sent as punishment for sundry adolescent crimes, yet all of them were marked with panged timidity when approaching the gate. While waiting for the post boy in the past, I usually arrived on the path earlier than the scheduled noon delivery so I could peruse what sifted through the reeds, but on this latest occasion I stood facing the house that appeared more ruinous than its age would suggest.

Its entire right half slumped on a crumbling column, as if the ravages of war had drifted this far downriver, but the yankees were too daunted by the prospect of swampland, and they had already conquered the city to the south. Cherubs carved into the bases of the columns seemed more like gargoyles unleashed to hunt in the swamp, possessing sharp incisors and youthful cheeks. As the sun burned the slimy enfeebled flow, its reflection was concentrated into a single glaring band of light anchored by the crooked edifice with its closed shutters and ravaged slates.

Looking southward down the road, the band of light shuddered with the approach of the post boy, the right half of his form indistinguishable from the liquid glare. I held two envelopes, one addressed from Louise to her sister in the city, and the other addressed to the archdiocese and bearing another request for a priest from Sister M.

The boy stopped more than an arm's length away, unbuckling his satchel and removing two envelopes and a carton of cigarettes. I stepped forward and held out the envelopes, but before the exchange was made he said he was supposed to ask if the post was cleaned, and I nodded, telling him not to worry, and he took the envelopes and handed me the newly arrived post.

Before the town upriver dared receive deliveries from the camp, they ensured that all materials were dipped in bichloride of mercury solution and left to dry. Sometimes the solution stained the ink so that the words faded, becoming almost illegible, and sometimes the parchment itself burned away, or became a translucent substance that was folded like wet cloth and slipped into the envelope.

After tipping his cap, he squinted at the house, swiping his feet in the dirt, and then headed back as the glare overtook the road. I shaded my eyes and walked across the road, perhaps with the same sheepish curtsy of that mortified boy. Through the gate I saw Sister M. nearly concealed by the porch's shadow, and I handed her one of the envelopes at the top of the stairs.

This one is addressed to the Mother, she said. It must be from the city parish. About the priest assignment.

I watched through the front window as she sat at her desk and hastily read the letter with a panged expression before I walked around the house to deliver the carton to the men's cabin and hand the other envelope to the grandmother who was in the garden scraping the rows.

She took the envelope and tore it open, reading the letter beneath the shade of the cabin's eaves. The stamp bore the city's seal, and I had assumed she came from the North, given her rigid vowels and rapid drawl, but then perhaps she migrated later in life, thus becoming infected by the tepid climes while residing downriver.

When I returned to the house, the parlor was empty. The letter addressed to the Mother was folded and tucked inside the ledger book. Through its bureaucratic obtuseness and seemingly inexhaustible arsenal of tallies, I was able to intuit urgency in the unsteadiness of its penmanship. The holding terminal, the letter claimed, was becoming overrun with patients as if an epidemic had beset the city, and the single doctor on staff was helplessly insufficient while the nurses had either been frightened off by the magnitude of new cases, or took to bed after collapsing from exhaustion, resulting in a mandate issued by the city officials that more holding terminal patients would be transported to the camp in the following months until some modicum of stability returned to the terminal. The letter also suggested that the camp would eventually quarantine most of the afflicted from this region of the nation. I scratched some figures on an old delivery slip, but I could not deduce the actual number of new patients expected to arrive.

On the second floor, I heard the plodding footfalls of Sister M., most likely inventing chores for herself to do so that fatigue would overwhelm any concern she had after reading the letter.

The patients had become accustomed to gradual changes in camp population, but they probably never expected a sudden, substantial increase of disoriented hordes arriving with unseen permutations of the affliction, stifling the air with their tubercular breath, their choleraic stool dribbling through the floorboards, tumbling across the cabin to wrestle for food, crowding the already trodden yard with their indolent gossip and wads of gelatinous spit. The doctor, already malarial and resented by some of the patients, would be endlessly summoned, probably hastening his return to the city, and we would be forced to house a number of the new arrivals in the cabin of Cybele and Ratherne, violating an early agreement made between the Mother and the sheriff to segregate the patients according to ancestry.

I folded the letter inside the envelope and hurried outside to help Sister E. pin linen, recalling Sister M.'s expectant gleam when she believed that word regarding the priest assignment had arrived. Although the holding terminal promised more souls to be delivered, they omitted any reference to an increase in supplies, which would require us to implement further rationing of our already plundered stock.

Before dinner was prepared, I rummaged through the parlor desk for the last delivery receipt and marked what remained in the kitchen. Another delivery of similar bulk could be expected in a fortnight, either preempting the arrival of the new patients, or arriving on the same barge, in which case the meager crates and barrels would be lost among the horde, consumed during the journey after the pilot dove overboard, while the sanitation employee cowered from the infected mutiny. The previous delivery consisted of the following:

4 pair hinges	1 box of nails
3 large spoons	10 lbs oats
1 bag of white beans	1 washstand
3 box of soda crackers	2 box of laundry soap
1 bolt of cheese cloth	8 lbs of split peas
1 bbl of cakes	10 lbs rice

After tallying up what I had counted in the pantry and the storage room, my gut quivered and I crumpled the slip in my pocket. More water had to be drawn from the pump, possibly requiring the well to be widened, or the construction of a cistern, and more cots and stools must be dragged from the storeroom and installed in the cabins. The patients would continue to bicker after we rustled off to the house, the strongest of them reapportioning morsels according to their whims. Our attentiveness as caregivers would be parsed thinner, shuffling from one crowded cabin to another with catheters and dressing kits, helping those in wheelchairs to slog through mud until the yard soon became overcrowded and the walkways busted. The scullery's hallowed instruments would be ruined with overuse and toppled to the floor by the helpless crowds, vials of sodium salicylate and strychnine stolen, lizards scampering from the shattered bowls, pages of notation shredded and soiled under the tide of writhing bodies. Sabbath would find the chapel riotous, pews collapsed through caved floorboards, Sister M. straining through her prayers over the cacophony until she fainted from her voiceless exaltations while tack would be wrestled from my grip, the crumbs swept up by those kneeling, wine guzzled from the jug, coughed up and trickling from their chins.

I stepped from beneath the canopy for the staunch morning rains, swallowing the heavy drops, a supplicant to the downpour, letting them saturate me without relenting to cold or the sliding earth. How foolish it was to speculate upon what the heavens intend, but the sensation of rain drenching my dress conveyed a greater presence, one that sought to comfort me and warrant my abandon but for a moment before I split more kindling for the parlor fireplace.

The taste of rain was more palatable than the cloudy water drawn from the pump. I wanted to believe in the permanence of its taste when the drops melded into the beastly swill of the river, that a trace of its unearthly sweetness carried through the water and each drop gleamed until the mud enclosed it. The earth was hidden from radiance, and I was called from my shelter to bow and drink, to honor my fortune by praising the miraculous, these glorious drops that pierce me and slake my irresolute spirit.

But wet kindling would serve no good, so I bundled up

the dead branches and held them beneath my arm while the canopy withstood the downpour, and the footpath became a forceful stream that ran into the flooded clearing.

On the porch of the men's cabin, Charles sat with a branch and rusted blade, teaching the boy how to whittle. He saw that I brought no food with me and clicked his tongue. The boy squinted at the blade.

Inside the cabin, the sergeant was asleep and Este was waiting for me in his wheelchair, not yet fully dressed. He said he didn't feel the burns until nighttime. Paul turned onto his side, grumbling admonitions to his cabinmate with the counterpane pulled up to his mouth. Following the doctor's request, we supplied the medicine in moderate drips to his breakfast. His fever diminished and his coughing became less severe. He nevertheless remained prostrate in his belligerent vigilance, slyly accusing us of poisoning him to suit the doctor, but he accepted food as if indeed the injections were affording him some glimpse of vigor, however much he nibbled and coughed, dropping his spoon to the floor, his unfinished meals immediately reclaimed by the sergeant who slurped up the remains.

I pushed Este past the pots set about the floor to collect what leaked through the roof. Across the trench, Ratherne stood beneath the matriarchal oak, almost unseen but for the glow of his pipe. Charles crossed the porch to help carry Este down the steps as the boy was circling in and out of the tumult unleashed by the eaves. Out in the yard, I lunged against the chair until my feet sunk, scraping mud from the wretched wheels, surprised by own strength considering how my spindly arms dragged with flaccid wings.

The steam contraption hindered the scullery door from fully opening, but steam still coursed outward, scattered by the downpour. The doctor was supplying wood, his shirt drenched, his cuffs brushed by ash, leaning into the fire and unaware of our entrance until I stood before him, drying my hands on my tunic.

The doctor told me he had awoken some moments before the first bout of thunder when the lizards enacted their panicked gyrations against the glass. He then asked me whether I wanted a cup of coffee brewed the day before although he must have remembered that I had always resisted his offers in the past. I can admit to the enlivening properties of the dark substance, its tinge forking through my veins, but my innards recoil during digestion, and I awaken the following day with a scowl and a pulsing brain.

We lifted Este onto the table where he undressed and the doctor helped me lower him into the tank. The lid was fastened and steam funneled through the hatch. I went to the desk to begin my transcription of the treatment, noting Este's silence as he was lowered into the tank.

The doctor approached the desk and asked if Paul was still receiving medicine in his food. I told him that the patient was suspicious of any food we gave him, but he was still eating his meals. The doctor lingered beside the examination table, watching the tank as the fire calmed. He said he had decided to no longer visit the men's cabin.

If he decides to apologize, I will await him here, he said. I know what my obligations are, but until he admits to his wrongdoing, I must assume he will attack me again. He carried two pieces of firewood from the oven to the tank and proceeded to poke the flames before grabbing his coffee cup from his desk and returning to the tank where he placed it on top to heat the watery grains.

If the disease infects the peripheral nerves, he said, then no one could claim unequivocally that the central nervous system is not also infected. You yourself, Sister, are surely aware of those medieval lazar houses where the afflicted were confined alongside the insane. The distinction that some of my colleagues would draw was hardly conceivable in the past. Both types of patients could be privy to hysteria, brash acts, sheer rottenness of character. I am not suggesting we regress to wholesale confinement. It is really a matter of anatomy.

He asked me if I had seen the admission warrant that

accompanies each patient, and I told him that I had. At the top of each warrant, the following was printed:

Afflicted
Description of ~~Insane Person~~ Named Below

The doctor conceded that the city health officials probably printed but one warrant, but he also wondered whether ancient fear should not be heeded, that is, the propensity for the afflicted to resemble the criminally insane in many cases should not be considered an archaic failure of medical science. We may have no need to consult leechdom manuals or diagnose ailments according to the disharmony of the humors anymore, he said, but the genius behind those arts is yet unsurpassed by the strides of our knowledge.

The steam no longer clouded the ceiling. Este was still silent inside the tank when the doctor lifted his cup from the lid. I set the pen down and kneaded my hands.

I have cared for lunatics, I said, and perhaps you have too, but the patients here are of an entirely different sort. Given to lies and gambling and childish fits, yes, but they are conscious of their vice.

But as caretakers, the doctor replied, we must admit to the parallel fates they spin among their own kind, all that we remain blind to because of our separateness.

When the doctor lifted the lid, I felt the sting within my tunic, and the collapsing cloud pulled at the pages. Este emerged from the tank, his flesh faintly branded, and sloughed hair from his back with his curdled fingers. Before the doctor or I could help to lower him from the table, Este attempted to stand up unaided, and his legs briefly wobbled before buckling just after he seemed to acknowledge that he was upright with a consternated smile. The doctor poked Este's thigh with his scalpel and asked him to report any sensation, but he claimed to feel nothing.

I sat bootless in the parlor divan, puzzling over the fate of Lazarus. I had been reading how the priests considered having the restored man put to death for fear he would attract more followers to the one proclaiming himself to be the Restorer. Yet Lazarus was allowed to live and returned home to care for his dour sisters, one of whom eventually washed the Restorer's feet with a luxuriant oil six days before his crucifixion.

Sister E. listened to me reading while she groomed her tabby, which occasionally rolled onto its back, exposing its engorged teats. Sister M. had completed her writing, probably responding to the letter from the holding terminal officials and fretting over the accounts. She told neither Sister E. nor myself about the news of the imminent arrival of more patients. She stood near the front window, saying how the Mother had foreseen our destruction before she died, and we deemed her to be feverish and ignored her ranting. She had been speaking of her own death, Sister M. said, and the evil it would bring to the camp. Sister E. replied that there was still enough food. The patients attend service and the cabins have not flooded, she said. But Sister M. scoffed at her and lifted the tabby, which was clawing gently at the hem of Sister E.'s habit, cradling it tightly.

Repentance will not safeguard anyone against sin, she said, before opening the door into the hallway and climbing the stairs.

Soon after, Sister E. bid me good night and retired to her chamber, possibly discomfited by being left alone with me in the parlor for she was accustomed to being alone with Sister M. after I had retired early. But on this particular night, I had not abstained from retiring to my chamber unusually late. Rather, our de facto Mother completed her affairs and pronounced her cryptic ruminations earlier than usual. Under the auspices of my solitary freedom, I could further recline in the soggy divan, outstretch my toes and relish in the expansive quiet of the parlor where the panels and frames became unsettled as if the spirits which staked their unruly inhabitance had become flesh and were promptly abandoning the house.

On the shelf, between a book of wretched hymns published by a convent in New Hampshire and a volume of St. Anselm favored by Sister M., was a work I had been most fond of since arriving at camp, a collection of canticles composed anonymously during the Middle Ages and translated some half a century ago by a yankee priest attached to a rectory in Cuba.

Since the canticles were dedicated to St. Ursula, they shared her name. Some of them reminded me of my beloved Ovid whose books were not permitted in camp because of their pagan implications. But the Latin poet is a more robust companion to camplife than most of the Gospel for he confronts decay and rejuvenation with a more brazen eloquence than most servants of God.

Since I was too wakeful to recall the day's minutiae, I wrote misremembered lines of Ovid:

> *As the wound on his foot meekly mends,*
> *Philoctetes curses the serpent,*
> *trails spools across cliffs*
> *this generation of godly rancor*
> *enticing man to banish and bid disgrace.*

> *Fissures of heaven spread*
> *and earth drains again*
> *beyond restoration of sacrifice,*
> *drowned oracles encrypt the fate*
> *of writhing molds soon enclosed*
> *in vines of coursing ore*
> *forged by the breath of Helios railing*
> *as their eyes palely emerge from fibrous scales*
> *and their fingers span from the curdled drip*
> *of simmering froth.*

Before the moon encloses,
she snaps a serpent's jaw
with her spells, uproots each stone
till the mountains yaw.
In trenches of sheepblood
she crawls to her altar of honey
and rapturous wind, drenched in milk
for the king of shadows please him
with stag liver and talons of ancient owls.

Rivers swept with all qualities of horror
infested climes rouse unrepentant
and south winds run cruelly
with fetid tongues through villages,
charred fields cursed by Juno's bile,
burning viscera hung from racks
at the storming of Aegina.

When I called on Cybele for her weekly dressing, the windows were papered, and the third cabin reeked of decay. The coals last stoked at dawn still cast light on Cybele bedded tightly.

Ratherne sat beside her, rubbing beneath her jaw partly unspooled of stained dressing, exposing strings of pus encrusted down her neck. I asked how many days she had been like that, and he lifted three fingers. Her eyes opened and she outstretched her hand to my voice. As I tried to lift her head and snip the old bandage, Ratherne refused to let go of her jaw as if he feared doing so may disrupt her breathing, or cause her mandible to unfasten and indeed the lower half of her face seemed almost severed, kept in its tenuous hold both by his fingers and strands of gauze.

I told him she must see the doctor, but he shook his head and stroked her face. I knew he must have left her alone in that condition on some occasions because I had seen him standing on the porch or beneath the oak, sometimes straying into the foliage, propped on his crutch, his gaze turned from the cabins.

I pulled closer to Cybele as Ratherne beckoned for me to utter a prayer, bending his head, still holding onto her. After finishing the prayer, I remained by her side on the cot, watching Ratherne's lips moving beside her ear, his eyes closed like hers.

In Cybele's case, the doctor's visit would not be beneficial. She had relinquished her willpower to her cabinmate, and in that dim and putrid cabin she wished to parlay with death beside the man who embodied mortal love for her. If her fate veered toward dissolution, then no medicine could dissuade it. The dirt had been cast and now one waited to see how it covered the ground, whether it would be marked with prophetic runes, blown upward once again or covered by yet more earth.

Because of the cabin's location furthest from the waters, and consequently from the house, Cybele should have had uninterrupted rest. I imagined how their cabin would transform after more patients arrived, what hostility would ensue as patients housed with those who had habitually been excluded from their company, how the cots would cram into the walls, piled atop one another, how the stench would intensify, and if Cybele were still bedridden, how such activity may jeopardize her condition.

I thought of asking Ratherne whether he had witnessed someone traipsing towards the house at night while he presumably stayed up with Cybele and lifted the covered window above her cot, drawing from his pipe and exhaling into darkness, but such a question during such a trying occasion proved inopportune. Later that evening I wondered whether Ratherne would ever betray another patient's petty crime to an outsider and why the disappearance of supplies would perturb him so long as he and Cybele had their portion. If any unspoken ban operates among the patients, it is that each nocturnal rambling shall be conducted in confidence.

What is etiology but damnation's province? One seeks after the cause of a malady when it is imbued with a mythic force, when the cure is still elusive and the ravaging persists. Theories behind the affliction's origin have consecrated a science of their own, an inexhaustible codex of persistent superstitions and grotesque anatomy, instruments of licentious shapes and recipes dreamt up by disgraced apothecaries. Some claim that infection is spread by repeated exposure to the scent of honeysuckle while others derive infection from contact with standing water. A few theories postulate hereditary causes wherein a strain occasionally bypasses certain generations, appearing more vigorous when it chances to return.

Medical apostles of late have rendered blame unto various animal species, most culprits being creatures who prefer night's domain such as possum or owls, while sometimes crickets and toads fall under the etiologist's scrutiny, and whether one must touch the creature or simply inhale its scent is often left unspecified. Outdated cures such as leeching were premised on a correspondence between the affliction and blood circulation, so that a body would be drained of infection and thus restored to purity.

In one of my visions, the corpse being pulled from the waters was nearly concealed by a host of leeches as though the river had sought to purify whoever stumbled into its grasp. According to those ancient pathologies the doctor referenced while Este steamed in the tank, certain diseases corresponded to various organs or external appendages and thus a leech would be placed upon a corrupt region so that the humors could once again achieve balance.

The vision must've prolonged my sleep, surfacing long after other dreams had washed away, for I slept until dawn. After getting dressed, I rushed downstairs to fill the furnace and found Sister E. hunched over the stove, her greeting replete with caustic cheer as if I had interrupted her wish to sing in solitude.

Heaven had once again been grateful with rain. After its lordly star emerged, each tuft of moss and stalwart acacia melted under the infernal swelter. The earth may be washed endlessly, its nethermost layers overturning and flushed riverward, but its scars still remain. Faint furrows that followed woodline, a geometric felling of vines and trees that left hectares of land where occasionally a cluster of stalks grew together, conspicuous and yet oddly at home in the flooded thicket. Perhaps birds had transported seeds from across the river where sugar was still harvested by unseen blades, or perhaps the scarce cane was a vestige of this camp's former incarnation.

According to the Mother, the former priest had sought to eradicate the stalks wherever they sprouted in the camp. Their appearance, she told us, reminded him of less humane epochs, and they stood as offense to his more compassionate leanings. With a scythe rummaged from the barn where the mill had once churned, he hacked through brush, just as he had done when searching for the corpse of the murdered patient. The Mother had seen canecutters on the other side of the river, working their way through the thick rows. At twilight, fathers would take turns sharpening their blades on a stonewheel spun by their sons. As a cloud of sparks leapt, she would strain to hear the screeching, but the distance was too great and her hearing too diminished.

I went to the well, figuring a little sweat beneath my underarms would be better than waiting until later on when the rain would return and drench me in the downpour. Some fifty yards down the road, I saw drab figures shuddering through the magnolia row. I unhooked the rope and let the bucket plunge, lifting my head to watch as I pulled it up. They emerged into light directly east of the well, a shirtless man leading a pack mule with flies trailing its caked haunch that teetered with every step under a bulk the size of an uprooted domain. Behind the mule walked a woman, her face shaded with pale cloth and neither her nor the man turned toward the well when the bucket splashed. Both of them were barefoot and dust climbed past the drowned levee's reach in darkened motes as the woman hurried ahead, more agile and possibly younger than her companion who favored his left leg as he rambled. Both appeared more entranced by their lulling path than the riverfront manor that melted in unison with the surrounding flora.

After the fourth bucket, I filled my load and hooked the rope back inside the well where at the bottom a beetle struggled to cross. I wished for a moccasin to emerge from the depths to end the beetle's crossing, some creature which subsists off very little and blends in hue with stone and water, a protector of those depths, its eyes watchful through blindness.

I hoisted the covering and looked down the road still clouded as Sister E. kneeled on the porch, scrubbing the slats, always willing to exert more in her servitude to Sister M. than myself and with a voice more enticing in its lamentations. She was not hounded by specters during her upkeep, and the road traffic did not disrupt her dedication. Perhaps she could not be alone with me in the parlor because she feared our difference would tend toward resolution. She would become less pure in her devotion, and I would become Sister M.'s more dutiful servant and preferred parlor companion, the one who worried each time she sniffled, who marveled at the intricacies of her exegesis, who lifted sacks and scrubbed floors to prevent her from ever bending her back.

In the yard, the grandmother was searching for Lucas to help her plant radishes. I went to the women's cabin and found him crawling before the washbasin curtain, following a mouse that was crawling beneath the floorboards. So enthralled was he by the creature's squealing that he did not notice me in the doorway. I heard water splashing behind the curtain, then Louise's voice telling Lucas to stop pounding the floor as he scrambled over a loosened board, deftly guiding around the stove until he arrived in the uncluttered pathway where he crossed my shadow and stood up and ran to me, trying to pull off my cornice. None of that today, Louise said, stepping from the curtain with her stomach rounded over her dark pelt. In her embarrassment she stepped back, but I could see her secret silhouetted through the frayed muslin, her bloated thighs and breasts, a shadowplay of caresses tending to the womb.

I told Lucas to follow me outside and led him down the porch steps. Of course my calling breeds naivety, which can never be completely offset by its apostolic strain. Our seclusion becomes so manifold that we presume virtue among all those under a godly roof, notwithstanding eruptions of treachery and vice. I was not as astounded by Louise's pregnancy as by her cunningness. So much chaff was made invisible.

I went to retrieve water for the garden, wondering if she had kept her secret from her cabinmates, a deception that seemed impossible to maneuver even for a woman who revealed nothing of her past save that she was once a seamstress and who shied from ever avowing her sincerest intentions.

Other than her scarred face, she displayed no outward signs of ever having the affliction, and the sergeant both scolded and envied her for it, as if she had been sent as some emissary swayed by science or faith to observe the camp's machinations, or to dwell among the afflicted as atonement for the unspoken indecencies of her former life.

Among the other men, however, she elicited an adolescent shyness. Less was known of Louise than both the grandmother and the girl although she had lived here thrice as many months. This was partly due to her unassuming air, her tendency to acquiesce to the camp's routine, as if her residence were an act of expiation, forever repeating her modest smile to the sergeant's accusations, or standing at the chapel's far wall during vespers with Lucas by her side.

In the afternoon after Este's steam treatment, I looked at her admission papers and revisited the record I had taken during the previous doctor's first and only examination of her, but the papers revealed nothing unfamiliar. City born, unmarried, privately employed. Compliance with authorities upon apprehension and captivity. Her hair was listed as red, but had since become darker. An auburn tone streaked in grey. Her date of birth was written beside a question mark. If she refused to divulge it, her form surely would not have read that she was compliant. In the doctor's report, she claimed to have little if no sensation around her face, neck, and shoulders, and her respiration was described as regular. She was listed as myopic, but did not wear spectacles.

She may have been just as suitable for steam treatment as Este, given her moderate symptoms. Perhaps the doctor favored her, or cherished her severe comeliness so much that he would not encase her in steam, choosing the hapless cripple instead. The doctor would seem an easy culprit to be paramour given that he resided in private quarters and could traipse about the grounds at night with more freedom and ease than the patients. But judging from her womb's girth, I put her pregnancy near halfterm, which would most likely put her conception around the time he was still packing vials in the city, eager to soon be rid of his colleagues.

The grandmother and the girl must have been aware of her added weight, her bouts of vomiting and dizziness. If so, they were complicit in Louise's deception and therefore must have been recompensed in some fashion. I could have asked Louise who the father was when she stepped from the basin, and she most probably would have told me, but embarrassment prevented me. My attention was trained to encompass all that occurred at the camp, and yet I was ignorant of a seismic event that had never occurred in the camp before, at least according to the Mother's enthralling yet assuredly inaccurate chronicle.

A purdah partitioned the men and women's cabins in the early years. The gouged earth was outfitted with a wire fence constructed by the sheriff's men. What they excelled at in apprehending suspects, they apparently lacked in engineering skills, and the first flood swept the fence riverwards. Only during Mass were both sexes permitted to occupy a single dwelling. The Mother must have believed that beneath such a roof and exposed to such words, the men would not lust while the women would languish under its holy force.

If Sister M. were privy to Louise's secret, her hysteria could have possibly reached a threshold upon which sanity was irretrievable if she were not already irretrievably mad. The doctor mentioned the patient's parallel fates during our conversation in the scullery, their propensity to withhold so much from the unafflicted, but I had no proof he was aware of Louise's secret. His statement could have been another gesture of diluted psychology, an effort by a herpetologist to forecast currents of the soul. However, if Louise or her cabinmates were to seek treatment, they would most likely first approach him since he embodied a disposition more secular in practice and therefore less judgmental where carnal impropriety was involved.

The cow lumbered into a faint blue mist that dulled the clang of its bell and collapsed onto its knees, occasionally lifting its head at strident thrushsong in the canopy. The mist brushed my face. I expected the doctor to step outside at that hour with his lizard sack and retractable net. I was sure the warmth had coaxed forth reptiles, enticing the doctor from his feverish hibernation, but the camp was quiet until Ratherne emerged onto the porch to smoke in his newly fashioned chair.

I crossed to the scullery where the doctor stood in the doorway, fitted with robe and slippers, inhaling steam from a basin. He lifted up his head and bid me enter, drying his face and pouring water into the tank.

During the course of the previous evening, I had postulated dozens of stratagems in which to snare him if indeed he had ravished Louise, but perhaps ravish connotes too much violence, the windfall of Jupiter upon mortal maidens. I considered bringing Louise to the scullery under the pretense of a routine examination, or staging a lascivious masque during our celebrations for Lent to capture his conscience, but all of my discarded stratagems bespoke of more conniving and cruelty than I was accustomed to, so I opted for parsimony and told him that a patient was with child. He did not blubber in denial, or edge me in malice, but peered inside his cup of dead ants and said his anole needed food or otherwise it would not leave its bowl.

It will outlast them all, he said, but first I must find it some companions. He shuffled from his desk, rubbing a soup stain from his lapel, and crossed to the fireplace to pick through ashes for his tin cup. He told me the women came to him months ago and said Louise wasn't bleeding anymore.

I told her it would be better to wash the fetus out, he said. Because of the frequency of her pain, and the discharge they have spoken about, it has little chance of being born alive and even then must be reared amidst affliction. She may be numb to touch, he said, but sensation speaks through her. She strops her cry so as not to waken the house. It's worrisome that the closer she comes to giving birth, the less severe her pain is.

And the father, I asked.

She does not speak of him, he said, and she refuses my help. She trusts no one.

He sat at his desk and stirred his cup, his face dripping onto the pages. She's strong, stronger than the others, he said, but she doesn't deserve any more punishment.

His assumption that we would discipline her bewildered me as if his creed were more equitable or beneficent than ours. I began to defend myself, but he interrupted me and said he did not regard me as punitive. It was Sister M. whom he feared might enact justice.

Her thoughts are elsewhere, I said. You have received news from downriver about the arrivals?

Yes, and Louise will be forgotten, he said. That would suit her wishes. If I were sent my centrifuge and microscope, I could give a better diagnosis, but now all of them are confused, resentful, stubborn with disease, and you and I, we teach them how to distinguish defeat from resignation. You are more able than I am, Sister, not because of your faith, or that you believe in an everlasting soul, but because for you evil may reside in all things. You are not here to cure anyone, or confirm your beliefs. You did not choose to be here, and therefore you doubt nothing, discard no illusions between here and downriver.

His neck flinched as he sipped from the scalding cup that he held with a rag. Before I went back to the kitchen, he asked me not to tell Sister M. about Louise.

She needs only rest, he said. The grandmother told me she tried cutting her wrists. She is a devout woman, but she does not think her faith will save her.

I told him Sister M. would discover eventually, but I agreed it should be concealed from her until after the delivery of the child.

From the front yard we could hear the engine turning. Sister M. seemed unabashed by her tears as she faced downriver. When she walked to the road, the billowing linen concealed all but her cornice. I stepped under the clothesline to follow her as smoke rose above the canopy. She knew the barge would wait for us, but she still hurried against the wind, and I turned around to whistle for Sister E., who was crossing the yard, lifting her tunic over the mud.

Before the boat had docked, Sister M. was questioning a young emissary about the supplies, and the emissary removed a receipt from his jacket. He seemed even younger than the one who had arrived with the doctor, but he could have been the same man, shaven and paler. Sister M. reviewed the receipt while Sister E. and I rolled a barrel across the plank. She said there are no more supplies than before, but the emissary was lugging a grain sack ashore and did not raise his head.

After we unloaded all the supplies onto the shore, we attended to the four arrivals. They were three men and one woman. The youngest of the men was on a crutch, rasping a Slavic tongue with a bandage around his neck. The other two men were insistent on walking unaided although both limped considerably. One was bald with a long coat and tattoos on his sunken chest while the eldest had faint scarring and a patched eye. He was shrouded in multiple garments and perspired heavily.

The woman was similar in age to Louise and wore rouge and powder. She walked beneath a parasol and appeared weary of her companions. She carried a gunnysack whereas each of the men had a suitcase.

We dispensed with all questions, learning in our first months that arrivals prefer to experience their introduction to camplife in silence. The emissary trailed behind us, rolling the barrel that continued to sink into the road until it became impossible to move. Sister E. and I carried the grainsack to the porch while Sister M. led the arrivals to their cabins.

We returned with a wheelbarrow to help the emissary dislodge the barrel, then fetched supplies for another hour, finding the pilot in all manner of diversions upon each trip back to the barge, either smoking in his cabin or wiping the windows, and when the deck was nearly emptied, he began to mop it.

The emissary could give us no word concerning the next batch of arrivals. After the plank and anchor were lifted, he said he would relay Sister M.'s request for increased supplies and tipped his hat with a grimace as the boat drifted away.

We finished stocking the kitchen with new supplies by dinnertime. Sister E. and I made rounds of the cabins with potato soup, first visiting the men's cabin where strife had already erupted over who was to have the last cot. The older man, who sat beside the oven, had blood dripping from his bottom lip onto his bandaged neck and clasped his suitcase to his gut while the bald man was unpacking his clothes beside the empty cot. The younger arrival had fallen asleep on the boy's cot, which mostly went unused since Lucas preferred sleeping on the floor, or in the women's cabin. The other cots seemed pushed closer together, thus isolating the two newly occupied cots.

The bald man had removed his jacket, revealing a tattooed pattern upon his back of what looked like interlocking shadows that transformed into serpent tongues as they wound tighter along his spine, which was unusually pronounced when he hunched over to untie his brogans. From his appearance he seemed healthy, but his gait as he walked along the river was unsteady, and I assumed his toes were severely afflicted.

Paul did not acknowledge his food and instead seemed

entranced by the tattooed pattern on the back of the new arrival, who turned away from the others as he ate, occasionally glancing at the older patient, his rival for the cot, whose hands trembled while he slurped his soup. Charles had his bad foot propped on a chair and told the old man he could sit on his cot since it was empty.

From the porch I watched Sister E. meet Ratherne in the yard with a steaming tray. She crossed to the women's cabin where I imagined her divvying morsels in the strained silence brought by the female arrival, who was probably removing her possessions from her gunnysack while the boy touched her vaporous hair.

With the empty tray tucked beneath her arm, Sister E. stepped from the women's cabin and crossed the yard to the kitchen where a gray cat was clawing at the door. She clapped her hands and hissed, but the creature reared with a stiffened tail and cried out until Sister E. lifted her boot, and the indolent creature, willing to sacrifice itself for scraps when the swamp that surrounds it teemed with food, jaunted from the stoop and returned to its brood, all of which had collected on the rise, reclining or sparring in crabgrass.

It warily approached the others and lowered its mangled ears before the fearsome tomcat, as if the leader had sent it on that foolhardy mission. The gray cat with mangled ears was an expendable scout not unlike the emissary sent to our camp with infected cargo, steered by a pilot whose face seemed hardened with vengeance against a river that had always tried to deceive him.

Paul had taken but a few spoonfuls when he passed his unfinished broth up to me and asked how a sick man could get better on such food. The young man with the crutch was still sleeping, and the other two arrivals gazed ahead as if still steeped in their former lives, hearing the din of carriages and fishmongers beyond the barred window of the holding terminal. The sergeant was humming what seemed like a martial melody, interspersing it with grumbled curses as if trying to provoke the new arrivals into a scuffle. He assumed Charles, the ablest of the men, would protect him, but the arrivals did not seem to acknowledge his dreadful rendition while Charles asked if Sister E. would sing alongside the victrola that afternoon.

He said he was tired of the sergeant's humming, and the poor fool had heard that song at cadet school because he had never marched in battle. When Charles wanted to lay back down, the eldest hurried from his cot and sat against the washbasin with blood on his hand from wiping his mouth.

I told Sister E. as she dusted the parlor about Charles' request, and we asked Sister M. if we could play music in the yard that afternoon. It was also four days before Lent would begin, and Sister M. decided in our favor, agreeing that music might soothe the newcomers whom she admitted appeared rather bewitched by their new surroundings.

We wheeled the apparatus across the kitchen and strained to carry it down the stoop. While I cranked the knob, Sister E. stood slightly askew from the row of cabins with her hands cloaked and her chin uplifted. The boy dashed towards us and leapt over the walkway, marveling at the spinning disc. The brass cylinder squealed for more than a few measures until the chorus was gradually heard, soon accompanied by Sister E.'s voice, which lured Charles onto the porch, followed by the sergeant and Este.

Her voice never rose above the recording, as if she were used to quieting herself before Sister M.'s voice during Mass. From the sweat dripping down my wrist, the knob kept slipping from my grip, and I gestured for the boy to take my place. He spun it with renewed spirit while Sister E.'s voice increased in pitch. The sergeant passed cigarettes to the other two men while the grandmother and the girl emerged from the women's cabin and sat on opposite ends of the porch.

The arrivals were not lured from the cabins by Sister E.'s voice, which began to break before the disc had stopped spinning. I went to the house and retrieved a cot from the storage chamber, asking for the key from Sister M. who was seated at her desk, penning another letter to the holding terminal with the new patients' admission slips beside her ink jar.

I dragged the cot inside the men's cabin, where the eldest arrival was asleep on the floor, resting his head on his suitcase. When I woke him and led him to his cot, he coughed and struggled to ask if I could write his wife. He said he had written her a letter at the holding terminal, but an orderly there had taken it from him.

The last time he saw her was when she had left for the dentist's. That's when they came to my house, he said. He leaned over the cot to rummage in his suitcase for a photograph of her, but his coughing was too severe. Before I left the cabin, the tattooed arrival told me not to trust what the eldest one said, especially whatever he said about him.

Sister M. and I unbarred the chapel doors for Mass and found Lucas asleep beneath the altar where the first priest had set up his own sacristy. The boy would not answer Sister M. when she asked him how he had gotten inside. She racked his rear threefold and he scampered to the corner, watching through his fingers as we arranged benches and swept the floor. Although he was malnourished and small for his age, he was not scrawny enough to slip between the chapel doors, which were admittedly bowed with rot, allowing for the occasional breach of rodents that were sometimes heard squealing behind the altar.

Sister E. brought tack and wine from the house and a votive was lit for our new arrivals, each of whom cautiously took their place on the benches. The bald arrival seemed either confused or scornful of Anaphora and when the eldest stuck out his tongue for tack, it was spotted with macules. Sister E. was too hoarse from her concert in the yard, and the men's deep timbre overwhelmed the women's voices when we sang from the Psalter.

Without the shade of her parasol, I could see that a form of leontiasis, or lion's face, had evidently struck the female arrival. Perhaps this particular condition was in its beginning stages for her eyes appeared symmetrical, but their blinking did not coincide, and she slurred her words when singing because her lips had wilted over her misshapen jaw.

Sister M. sipped from the ladle and we sat in silent prayer. She did not extend words of welcome or invoke God's watchfulness. Perhaps she felt such concluding rites belonged to a priest, or perhaps she knew just as they did that the camp was a place more worthy of forewarning than welcome. She herself would not stand outside the chapel doors like the Mother once did, kissing their cheeks and holding their hands. She was either too proud or too meek to usurp a priest's stature, so she turned towards the lithograph with its peeling edges while her congregation rose from their benches or wheeled across floor, some coughing, others retching with hunger and shielding themselves against the sun. After they had returned to their cabins, Ratherne limped up the aisle, dropped his cane and kneeled before Sister M., who had since turned from the faded lithograph.

I brought the arrivals' delivery forms for the doctor's perusal before he began his initial observations. When I placed them on his desk, I dreaded reading them for I preferred the patients to be as they were on the first day, nameless and without history, the signs of their affliction mostly covered by their garments. If I had learned more about their personhood, I would have been more compelled to pity their condition, but I viewed them as anonymous vacationers who had not yet calculated the length of their stay, transients whose alarming ailments had not yet been properly diagnosed.

As he followed me to the dooryard, he said he had visited Louise's bedside the previous night. He had told her he could do nothing to ease her pain besides administering morphine, which he hesitated to use for risk of addiction. According to him, the new female arrival began to beg indecently for morphine after seeing him inject Louise with a mild dose. After he asked her what was causing her pain, she grabbed his hand and placed it on her misshapen head, and he could feel it throbbing.

He told her it was probably fatigue, and she supped a tincture of salicylic acid. All of his analgesics were kept on his medicine shelf except for his vial of morphine, which was probably kept in his bag, or hidden somewhere in his quarters, the mighty substance within close reach as he writhed viciously on his soaked bed during his malarial outbreaks.

He thanked me for not confiding in Sister M. about Louise's secret. I wondered why Sister E. had not done so either since she was assigned general watch over the women's cabin and surely must have discovered it as well, but she was just as scared of Sister M. as the doctor was. From the doorway, he called out to the grandmother while she lugged a bucket across the yard, her head fixed downward. She set the bucket down on each step as she climbed to the porch of her cabin. They scoff at me when they don't need my attention, he said, closing the door as he stepped back inside.

Before the other women had completely awoken, the grandmother was sitting on the porch, threading scraps of newspaper and calendars with twine. After they had eaten breakfast, the other patients began helping her prepare for the celebration. Sister M. expressed surprise they had remembered the date. In years past, the celebrations were ignored because winter had demolished any festive proclivities by confining many to their beds with pneumonia.

Charles and the sergeant were boiling some molasses with fermented grain, the name of which they would not repeat in my presence although it seemed to cause much merriment among them. On the table hibiscus blossoms were spread out, which the men intended to brew with wine. Sister M.'s suspicions over where they had retrieved such materials were quelled during these preparations, but it must have only strengthened her belief that Charles was the pantry thief.

The grandmother was mixing herbs and beans at her stove while the girl stood on a chair and pinned paper bunting the grandmother had made from the porch rafters, after which she fashioned masks of twine and hickory leaves and walnut necklaces while Louise sewed capuchons with buttons pinned to their peaks.

Those who prepared for the celebration did so with quiet impunity as if they assumed we were forbidden from interrupting the sacred culmination of Lent, but in truth our rule over the camp relied on the patients' faith in our closeness to divine charity. Apostates who dwelled among us could celebrate each night as if it preceded a long spell of fasting and contrition, and we could not impede them. What we sisters compensated with rigor, we lacked in forthrightness. It was after all the priest with his particularly mellifluous tongue who coaxed the murderous patient into his bindings. Otherwise, the murderer could have absconded, or taken other patients hostage and ruled over the camp until some missive requesting help made it to the city, and the authorities arrived from downriver.

Sister M. did not ask aloud from where this newfound desire to celebrate had arisen and even asked Sister E. to make a batch of strawberry marmalade for the occasion. She had to accept their cause for festivity because they outnumbered us and could have easily dictated their own routines, gorged as they wished, lounged about in the house in splendid solitude until they descended into the parlor to writhe before the lit fireplace, doting upon their own decay after we were summarily banished to the waters while all our receipts and ledgers smoldered atop the levee.

I was tasked with leading the new arrivals to the scullery for their observations. When I fetched the younger one with the crutch, he was scraping a file over his nails, grinning with watery eyes, which made me suspect he was in a stupor due to inhaling fumes from the simmering spirits, but he complied politely and followed me across the yard.

While the doctor examined him, he was surprised to discover that the young man's limp was the result of his knee being crushed beneath a wagon wheel, not from any affliction that had spread to his leg. When the doctor asked him how the accident occurred, he confessed he had fallen asleep in an alley after being robbed by his brother-in-law. He said he told his sister not to marry an American because they're all crooks, but overall he seemed amused by his misfortunate account, smiling drunkenly until the doctor drew closer, after which he lapsed into his mother tongue, presumably cursing the doctor who wielded a scalpel above his bare leg.

Of his knee all that could be seen was a knob of pulp, which must have gone untreated for months. The orderlies in the holding terminal must have also assumed that his limp was attributable to the affliction, which had spread to his face. His breathing was regular and any painful sensation from his injury was lost to him so that the doctor could jab at what remained of his knee with a scalpel without eliciting even a wince.

His delivery form put his birthdate seventeen years prior and listed Prussia as his place of birth. However, the language he spoke was not German, and he claimed his birthplace to be Hrvatska. Not only had the authorities at the holding terminal mistaken his country of birth, but the empire in which that country was located. Men of that country are renowned for their nautical craftiness, and indeed the young man had a bronzed face and his hands appeared strong even if some fingertips were scabbed and his palms were blistered.

My sister told me her fiancée was rich, he said, before slipping into his mother tongue with mocking gestures. Yes, I told her, he's rich because he steals from everyone, but he won't be rich in hell.

His grin became almost lascivious as the doctor combed through his long black hair for lice. As he was getting dressed, I asked him to take on another name while residing in the camp. He wished to be called Philip, a variation of his given name and the one he went by downriver, but I told him to choose a name he had never been called before, and he crossed himself with clenched jaw, spit spraying through his prayers.

Next, I brought in the tattooed man, who was, according to his papers, also a mariner, but ten years older, and who went to see a doctor for a fever while at the city port and was apprehended as he left the doctor's office to return to his boat. Like Charles, his feet were severely afflicted, but otherwise he appeared healthy since his fever had dissipated.

The doctor tested his vision after noticing discoloration of his sclera and asked him how he was fit to work at sea when he was nearly blind, but he scoffed at the doctor and said he didn't need eyes to man the riggings. He refused to undress but rolled up his trousers and seemed mistrustful of my tunic rustling behind him. The doctor's prized anole was scaling the ceiling, basking in the lamp that hung over the examination table, but the arrival could not see the creature dangling over him.

As he unrolled his trousers and sat up, he told the doctor he wasn't going to take any medicine. The last crank drugged me something awful, he said, so I couldn't fight back when those bastards came to take me, but the doctor assured him he had nothing of that sort in mind.

Does that mean I'm not sick, the arrival asked.

No, quite the opposite, the doctor answered, excusing the arrival from the scullery. With a grin not unlike the lame Croatian's, he watched the lizard cling to the lamp.

If the mariner entered the scullery with mistrust and obstinacy, he left it in an altogether timid state, asking me on our way back to the men's cabin when the doctor would let him leave the camp. It seemed this uneasiness was precisely what the doctor intended by withholding aspects of the arrival's condition and excusing him from his office with a suggestion of indefinite confinement. The doctor might as well have meted out a death sentence to the mariner. When I told him that no date had been given for his release, and that the doctor would have to examine him again, he stopped before the cabin and straightened his shoulders and said he swore he didn't have what the doctor said he had.

Every man in my trade's got something, he said. We come across lots of people. Lots of places. He said that locking him up wouldn't make him better.

I had a fever is all, and this is what rigging does to your hands after awhile.

He insisted that he did not belong in the camp, that he was not infected with anything more than scurvy and what he called sailor pox. I told him I had no say as to how long he would be confined, but it was as if he wanted me to offer him some incontrovertible evidence that he was afflicted, some divine signature writ over the doctor's own words. I could say nothing to calm him and left him pacing through the cloud of boiling spirits that hovered in the men's dooryard.

With the older arrival, the doctor was even more obscure in his diagnosis. While he was examined, he asked me again about writing to his wife, and I promised him I would transcribe his letter after the doctor was finished. The man was undoubtedly afflicted, but he must have resisted going to the doctor for years, possibly dismissing his wife's concern. His form claimed his occupation was repairing clocks and watches, and he said his wife dealt with the customers when his face would erupt with lesions. Because of his age and the living conditions at the camp, the doctor knew that his probability of surviving the summer was scant, but the eldest arrival never inquired as to his condition as if he knew of its severity. After the doctor tended to his split lip, the old man got dressed and told me what to write to his wife. He asked when the letter would be delivered and if it would first pass through the holding terminal. He wanted to sign the bottom, and I assisted him in holding the pen.

The doctor told me to next bring the female arrival as supper hour approached, and she walked into the yard with her parasol before her face although the sun was waning. She dashed past the gaze of Charles and the sergeant, who both smoked on the porch.

They seemed enthralled by her in a way that was different from their attraction to Louise, as if their curiosity were more piqued than their loins. It seemed the combination of her parasol, her lack of courtesy, and her unusual face lent intrigue to her persona, and the fact that she sought to dispel it with increasingly brash behavior had the effect of further enticing the two men.

The doctor appeared intrigued as well by the feline angularity of her face. He measured it and tested its sensitivity, noting its iridescent tone, her sprawling eyebrows and button nose. Six and twenty years of age. Birthplace unknown. Transported from a hospital in Florida, a place that seemed to me as alien and distant from camp as the fabled ivory streets of Lima.

To the question of what station she had occupied in her previous life, she answered wife but wore no ring and said her husband was glad to be rid of her. She complained of having a headache, and the doctor noted a pronounced throbbing in her forehead. He surmised that because of her skull's deformed growth, circulation to her brain had been constricted.

She was facing away from the medicine shelf, but she repeatedly turned around to look at the labels, telling the doctor that her husband would work her till her feet bled. But he never left me unsatisfied, she said. The doctor did not concede to her lascivious charm, advising her to drink more fluid, as if to save the morphine for himself. She pulled up the straps of her blouse and likened the doctor to those sons of bitches at the hospital.

Same ugly looks. Same dirty fingers. The sick leading the sick, she hissed.

I stood up from the desk and tried to calm the woman, resorting to the comforts of my creed, asking her when she was born, then telling her of the saint who attended her first birth, guessing it were Januarius, but later when I consulted the calendar, I realized I was mistaken. She laughed at the thought of being named after a month and relented to my touch, the parasol clenched between us. The doctor returned to his desk, and I led her into the yard where the boy tapped a dance on the walkway slats, and the other patients lingered on the porches, more boisterous than usual and impatient for feeding.

On the morning of the celebration, when we brought porridge and apportioned each patient a slice of shortbread with marmalade, the boy stood in the yard hurling the dinner bell over his head. In the men's cabin, Charles and the Croatian had already begun to celebrate, their linens and undershirts stained with liquor and tobacco juice, cajoling the sergeant to awaken. Paul's cot was empty, and I asked Charles where his cabinmate had gone. He said Paul went outside with his bedpan. When he returned later, he was seemingly lively of spirit and sipped from the Croatian's flask before devouring his breakfast. I had suspected him of exaggerating his condition of late, but I would be surprised by how much he had deceived us regarding its severity.

The men had burnt cork and piled it atop the oven. Later they drew with it on their faces, and Paul draped himself in muslin and pinned scraps of burlap to his capuchon and some of the other men donned masks made for them by the women. We pushed the victrola into the yard, but rain soon forced us to carry it inside the kitchen where its music was nearly lost to the noisome souls parading beneath the downpour.

I brought out the fiddle after the eldest arrival attested to playing the instrument, but his fingers were too afflicted so he plucked the strings with his teeth while the female arrival did a merry quadrille on the porch, her face smeared with powder and rouge. During those intervals of respite between storms, the victrola was brought back into the yard, and Este tossed rice and millseed from the porch onto those dancing in the mud. Charles had made a castanet from a tin can with a pecan inside and rattled his instrument, pulling himself atop the cow, which reared its head and bellowed with strain while the other men laughed.

Paul was dressed as a kind of hussar, wearing a coat with tatters pinned to the back and above his upper lip he had a moustache scrawled in pitch. He goaded the cow with a switch, choking on his liquor as he laughed, but the creature collapsed upon the mud, and Charles removed his capuchon, fitting it between the cow's ears.

In the beginning of the celebration, their methods of adornment were distinguished according to sex. Soon, however, the men gave their masks to some of the women, including Louise who did not conceal her stomach from Sister M. and instead seemed to flaunt it during the celebration, similar to how the female arrival decorated her face, or how the sergeant displayed his spasmodic toes to the amusement of the arrivals.

Sister M. would pull her rocking chair out to the stoop and sit down during the dry spells and would return to the house when rain commenced. Due to either her distance from the parade, or the general fanfare and jostling of bodies, she did not notice Louise's added girth until the day after when clouds had been drained and the battered earth, which had trickled down the rise, pooled around the walkway and leaked through the trellis of the men's cabin.

Perhaps because of the spirits that were consumed, the patients did not ask about their midday meal. When supper arrived, they scraped their plates clean and resumed guzzling liquor and altar wine while Sister E. and myself largely resided in the house, occasionally emerging to see what had incited their rowdiness, or to gather discarded garments and furniture which they had borrowed for the occasion.

By late afternoon, the doctor had emerged from his keep, lingering at the edge of the festivities until he was given a mask and capuchon and asked to dance by the female arrival, but dancing to choral music and a throbbing castanet proved too difficult for him, and he removed his mask, retreating from the parade to the porch of the the men's cabin.

After the doctor's appearance in the yard, Paul became more frenetic and even hostile towards the other men, trying to carry Este on his back up the rise, or swiping his switch at Charles in a mock duel. Soon, he became exhausted and stumbled up the steps of the men's cabin, swaying across the porch, his switch snapped in his fist. From where I stood across the yard, he looked to be trying to persuade the female arrival, who was sitting on a stool, to dance with him, but mud from his face dribbled onto her dress, the finest one she owned, and she stood up and slapped him. Charles grabbed Paul from behind before he could accost the woman and must have convinced him to go inside the cabin. As he passed the doctor, he looked over at him, but I could not tell whether he said anything.

Around nightfall, the doctor returned to the scullery. The mariner and the Croatian made a fire from slats they had upended from the walkway. Sister M. did not leave the house again while Sister E. stood beside the cabin steps, singing hymns to the tapping of utensils on the steps, the boy clanging the dinner bell while Charles limped around the burgeoning flames with his face caked in sweat and powder, rolling his fingers on the fiddle's backside and humming to himself the melodies that Sister E. intoned while the Croatian and the mariner blew spittle onto the fire.

Ratherne did appear at all during the celebration. Cybele's condition, after fluctuating starkly for weeks, had been lately improving. In the days preceding the celebration, she was able to move about her cabin, employing her cabinmate's cane to anchor her weight. Inside their cabin no light had shone and before I knocked I heard Ratherne push a stone away from the door with his cane.

I asked when they had last eaten, and Cybele said that Ratherne had stewed turtle with some roots. My lantern was lowered from his face, but I could see that he would flinch at any boisterous eruption from across the camp. I had not seen either of them venture from their cabin more than once or twice since the arrival of the new patients.

She told me that her breathing fits had almost gone away, and Ratherne had redressed her face. In their increased isolation, they had become more sensitive to what occurred outside their walls, which must partly be a consequence of their double banishment. Any visitor was cautiously vetted before entrance, and any noise that did not seem to emanate from the surrounding foliage was perceived to be an invasive spirit sent to wreck their solicitude. I doubted whether my presence in their cabin was welcome, as if they were already in mourning for their arcadia beneath the dogwoods.

Perhaps they mistrusted my intentions and wondered if I were partial to this conspiracy of outsiders who would soon trickle into their sanctuary and set up habitation in burgeoning numbers, a fate they must have loathed to fathom. The night of the celebration was yet another omen of their idyll's end. All the envy and misgivings they withstood during their tenure would become more forceful with an increased population, and their conjugal intimacy would soon be disrupted.

I dimmed the lantern on the porch of their cabin. The campfire appeared much farther away than it was. Trampled weeds and soaked ruts and sprigs all receded into its glow. Sister E.'s voice had quieted and the tapping of utensils and men's humming had absolved into rustling foliage.

Against the light, the boy ran towards the chapel, no longer holding the dinner bell. I unlatched the doors and called out his name. I heard rummaging among the altar and walked down the aisle and saw him crawl out from the platform where the first priest had his sacristy.

As with discovering Louise's secret, I was almost disgusted by my own ignorance. Just a few days prior Sister M. and myself had caught the boy inside the chapel, but we had not inspected the altar, which contained mostly empty potato sacks and wine vats.

The boy was aware of my temerity and did not tremble when I held the light to the mostly devoured store of supplies. He told me he stole them because the ladies told him to. It seemed he had been slipping through the back window of the house to steal supplies. Whenever Louise had a sweet tooth, or the grandmother needed more ingredients for her meals, which would in turn be shared with the male patients, he was then told to retrieve them from the chapel. Therefore, any accusation of thievery could have been leveled against all the patients, since each of them consumed the stolen supplies.

I had never shared Sister M.'s zeal in apprehending the thief. For her, the stealing of supplies had violated charity and was therefore a grievous transgression. This belief she inherited from the Mother, who insisted that each patient reciprocate the good deeds shown to them according to their ability, which is why some of them occupied themselves with tasks and tended to the upkeep of their cabins. However, one could claim that charity is defined by its lack of recompense and those of the apostolic creed give purely of themselves until their generosity withers away.

Since I was first to discover the looted goods, I was left with the responsibility of informing Sister M, who would then decide on the suitable repercussions. The boy was an instrument exploited by his elder compatriots while Charles had been a pawn in Sister M.'s mistrustful imagination.

I escorted the boy from the chapel, allowing him to take half a sack of meal to the women's cabin. Following along the edge of the house, I saw the fire still in full force. All the women save for the new arrival, who was shuffling with Charles on the porch beneath a wool blanket, had returned to their cabin. Paul had slept off his stupor and was crouched on the walkway, or perhaps it was another patient turned away from view, still wearing a mask.

My memory could have replaced another patient with Paul to somehow account for what happened later. He could have been curled up in his cot, unchanged from the position he had held for weeks, weakened by the doctor's tincture, or staring at the rafters, recollecting his failed escape, fashioning more tactful stratagems, better disguises. I would tell Sister M. later about seeing Paul in the yard the night of the celebration, about discovering that the stolen goods she so fervently sought were stored beneath her feet as she sermonized to those souls who had deceived her.

When I returned to the house, the parlor was empty. St. Anselm's 'Proslogian' was opened on the divan. I assumed that Sister

M. found comfort in his crystalline proofs for the existence of God, and she could hear each axiom resound in her mind, unscathed by the backyard din. Before closing the book and setting it on the shelf, I held it to my lantern. If there were a message being conveyed in those opened pages, it was indecipherable to me.

Sister E. stood before my door with a strained face while I was still in my nightdress. Paul did it again, she said. Immediately, I assumed Paul had attacked the doctor again, maybe this time with more destructive means. He left last night, she said. That's what the men say.

Paul had blessed us with his escape, but he had also damned himself. Although he was perhaps exaggerating his condition, he still was not fit enough to track through swampland for days on end. If someone were to discover him within close proximity of camp, they would have probably interpreted his oral disfigurement as a sign of affliction and reported him to the police. Paul knew he would most likely face recapture or death if he absconded, but this knowledge would not prevent him from trying it again.

Sister M. rang the dinner bell from the back stoop to signal a patient's disappearance, but we did not begin our admittedly shallow search until late afternoon. He had left his belongings, and no one witnessed him leaving. The Croatian had fallen asleep in the yard, a batch of ants clung to his bandaged leg while the mariner was slumped on the porch beside an empty jug. Inside the cabin, Este and the sergeant were jeering at Charles who had lipstick smeared on his face and beside his cot was a lace stocking worn by the female arrival. She must have scurried across the trench when Sister E. first caught them sharing a cot.

The eldest arrival was muttering about the couple's indecency, and how he had complained to them about their commotion throughout the night. Since the eldest arrival was awake at that late hour, I asked him if he remembered seeing Paul in his cot, but the old man said he did not remember. He thought he heard voices in the yard, but the couple's commotion was too loud for him to be certain.

While Sister M. inquired in the women's cabin about Paul's whereabouts, she asked Louise to follow her to the chapel where she would lead her in atonement. Let your sins be judged by a forgiving hand, she said. She was not bristling with condemnation as I had expected, but forestalled her own judgment, and calmly led Louise by the arm. I went to the third cabin and asked Ratherne whether he had seen or heard Paul the night before. Cybele translated for him and told me he had seen light beneath the doctor's door, but he had fallen asleep by the window, and the door was dark when he awoke.

I knocked before stepping inside the scullery. The wind had not ransacked it. It was the work of animal intent. Desperate calumny. Papers furled from the desk. The boiling contraption toppled, water spilled over the floor. Some of the glass vials and bowls were shattered, and the doctor's prized anole clung from the rafters while the other lizards were gone. The oven was cold. He had left with his robe, but his boots were beside the door, and his linens tousled.

I gathered pages from the floor: sketches of lizard eyes and tails, extracts from his manual on respiratory infections interspersed with the phrase, *She asks the moon for courage*, a tally of breathing frequencies and another fragment, *To break bread with captors, to be ruthless at the feast*, renderings of mothwings and antennae done with the same lackluster precision, graphs of ailments with corresponding treatments that were repeatedly marked over, a list of names, colleagues possibly, or patients he had treated in the past. Pages filled with illustrations of other contraptions, one with an aphorism, *What can stave the mud's hunger but the innocence of life*, a draft of a letter addressed to someone whose relation to the doctor could not be discerned from the cryptic missive, which continued with the same aphoristic tone, never referring to the addressee, but describing instead gradations of wind throughout the day, cloud patterns, feeding schedules for his lizards, a list of night sounds, measurements of rainfall, and at the end of the letter, which ran for some three pages, the doctor wrote, *Yours faithfully*, but left it unsigned.

The following page was a cursory map of the camp with much attention given to the surrounding overgrowth, various trenches and hovels, the curvature of the river. This constrained world we inhabited, no wider than a brittle page. But his world was wider than ours, he knew of gullies and paths I had never seen, had measured watercourses and rendered them to scale.

Scattered on the floor were pages torn from his books with portions underlined or circled, shreds of envelopes used as scraps for lists and diagrams, and drawings of human parts isolated from bodies, some apparently afflicted, some beset with other unknown deformations, faces at oblique angles with elephantine features, limbs dwarfed or contorted or spotted with lesions either rendered with hasty markings or left entirely empty. The people in his drawings were unrecognizable and may have been his patients at the university hospital, or vagabonds he had studied on the city streets, but a patient's identity was only important to him insofar as it demystified their affliction.

I swept the shards into a dustpan, scraped dried mud off the floor and walls, tidied up the bed, and set the steam tank upright before I told Sister M. about our second vanishing of the morning as we stood before the empty chapel. She was not convinced that both disappearances were connected and insisted on Charles' culpability in the matter. I told her the women's cabin had reported hearing shouts during the early morning, similar to what the eldest arrival told me, but the women figured it was the drunken men still celebrating around the fire.

I bid her to follow me to the altar and pushed back the board. She saw the sacks chewed by rats and empty tin cans. The boy was stealing for the women, I said.

She demanded I explain why I had waited to show her. You

knew about Louise as well, she said, staring at the altar.

She wished to punish me for my deceit, but she also knew she relied on my presence in the camp more at that moment than ever before. Instead of assigning me more tasks as punishment, she told me to comb the swamp, affording her more hours alone in which she could pontificate to her tabby about the mayhem that surged all around her.

With the doctor's map in hand, I followed his path for lizard collecting until the swamp was too thick to cross and rested against a leafless sycamore that slumped over a trench. The likelihood of finding traces of either man depended on what occurred in the scullery, on who initiated the struggle, and whether one of them was held captive and forced into the night against his will. Given Paul's previous assault on the doctor, it would seem that the roles of captor and captive were quite certain. The struggle after all did not occur in the men's cabin, but in the doctor's lodgings. Tracks were discerned in the mud, but I was confused by the endless monotony of trees doubled in water and soon realized they were my own. If the two men had crossed through the swamp, the mud had swallowed their traces, and if they had shouted from high ground, the trees had dispersed their echoes.

Sister M.'s panic became more intolerable after the celebration. She insisted on a full inspection of the grounds to uncover any contraband or stolen supplies. Because her trust in those she had been charged to care for had dwindled considerably, she assigned both Sister E. and myself to take turns with nightwatch over the cabins and demanded Charles fit the kitchen door with a lock, but he did so only after Sister E. asked him with her lilting, coquettish voice. He would take on any carpentry task to endear himself further to his celibate muse. Their affection for one another had become almost indecent since the celebration. Yet I was so slavish to the Lord's munificence, and His light had so pruned my heart that any human tenderness seemed inauspicious, even obscene in its desperation.

As punishment for the theft of supplies, Sister M. reduced the amount of each meal, but the patients did not threaten mutiny as if they felt worthy of rationing, especially during Lent. The door to the scullery was latched, and all of Paul's belongings were stored in the house. We removed the linens from his cot and washed them in preparation for another arrival, and when we returned it to the cabin, the other men slid their cots further away from it.

The grandmother and the girl planted a larger crop in their garden while the boy was instructed to forage for nuts and berries. The rest of the women were accompanied in the cabin by Sister E., who sang with them, and took up sewing in place of Louise who had become weaker after partaking in the celebration. To aid against her excessive sweating and palpitations, the grandmother brewed a tea of hackberry and witch hazel.

None of the patients bemoaned the doctor's absence. Sister E. or myself could do all the dressing and stitches. The camp had persisted many a month without a doctor in the past. But I knew we would see how valuable his residence truly was after the next batch of patients arrived, or if another disease spawned from the affliction and set forth to overwhelm us.

At night I listened to Charles and the sergeant gossip about Paul's whereabouts. The reason you can't find them in the woods, the sergeant said, is cause they took a boat to the city so the doctor could show him off, do more experiments on him. City's where you should look for them.

Charles laughed and said those two men wouldn't get on the same boat lest they were shackled together. If Paul went anywhere, it'd be downriver, that's where he'd run off to the first time.

I told them that Sister E. already searched the banks.

On both sides, Charles asked. I saw Paul swim the length of it when he was drunk once.

But he was too dizzy to swim, the sergeant said. The doctor got him weak with poison and took him on a city barge.

He wasn't too messed in the head, Charles said. One of them will come back. Then we'd know at least the half of it.

The mariner asked why the doctor would wait till that night to take Paul to the city, but the sergeant did not answer, as if he deemed a new arrival unworthy of answering. The eldest arrival rose from his cot and said everyone else was wrong. He alone knew what happened between the doctor and Paul.

That whole day Paul danced with every woman here, even that pretty Sister, but he didn't dance with the pregnant one, didn't even talk to her, or look at her, the eldest arrival said, then gestured to the other men and said all of them acknowledged the pregnant one except for Paul.

When the eldest arrival stopped to regain his breath, I thought about Paul stumbling on the porch during the celebration, getting slapped by the female arrival for something he had said to her. Louise was sitting on the porch, but closer to where the doctor stood.

Only one man would avoid a woman like that, the eldest arrival said. That's the man who loves her.

You saying Paul gave her that child, Charles asked. He weren't right in his head, but it weren't cause of love.

The sergeant, as if finally conceding to the enfeebled man's presence in the cabin, asked about the doctor. He loved her too, the eldest said, hacking more spittle into his bedpan. Aren't but two reasons why they'd skirmish and run off, love or money, and we all know there's no money to be had here.

As the eldest arrival continued with his theories, I marveled at how he seemed to exercise energies habitually devoted to clocks toward the amorous travails of his fellow patients, foreseeing reactions and intuiting causes while cramped in his cot, similar to how he had adapted his musical ability to playing the fiddle without the use of his fingers. The men continued to gossip about what had happened, the speculations becoming more fanciful purely for the sake of amusement until Louise, the doctor, and Paul became stock characters conniving out of jealously and lust, each repelled and enchanted by the limits of their malice.

The vision of the body being dragged from the river and prodded with a sounding pole claimed me with more ferocity. I sunk up to my knees in mud, pulling myself atop a log that also began to fill with mud until it cracked open. The river trailed silently, its gleam branded a stripe across the dark sky. The body, faceless and stained with silt, was kicked over the raft and engulfed by bubbles. While the earth entangled me in my sleep, I heard the men rasping their cynical suppositions as if I were still in the cabin on nightwatch.

In the swamp, with an axe as my armament, I hacked looping pathways that edged closer to the water. I left portions of my dress dangling from branches to serve as markings for my path and to alleviate the fabric's chafe. At dusk, after clearing another hectare of swamp, I met Sister E. on the backstoop where she was waiting to replenish my canteen. She was told by Sister M. to discontinue her search of the riverbank. She had trekked it thoroughly, she said, southward into town and northward to the makeshift jetty.

I washed my face and hands at the kitchen basin before preparing supper. When she entered the kitchen to tally supplies, Sister M. did not ask me what I had found during my search. She knew I had found nothing, and my punishment resided in the very futility of scanning the swamp.

Faith reminds us that the spirits we seek appear to us of their own volition, indifferent to our tireless search. The girl was the first to see the doctor and hollered from the yard. He walked unsteadily down the rise in clothes that seemed much too small for him, bearded and hatless, with a flushed forehead and a sack over his shoulder. Soon the other patients emerged from their cabins and watched him cross the yard. He stopped at the backstop, staring at us with a stranger's incredulity.

I saw the smoke coming from your chimney, he said. Otherwise, I would've walked all night.

The patients who gathered on their porches were watching the rise as if they expected Paul to reappear as well, newly dressed and shaven, perhaps even completely cured of the affliction. From where they stood, I wondered if the patients could also see that the doctor wore Paul's shoes, which must have partly accounted for his uneven gait. When he returned for supper after he changed into his own clothes and washed up, he had little to say of his whereabouts during the previous days. He told us a man found him and brought him home where his wife and daughter cared for him. When he was well enough to leave, they gave him food and water for his journey, but they knew nothing of the camp and could only tell him how to get to the river.

Although his appetite was strong and he answered our questions convincingly, his bearing was not altogether sound. His hand trembled as he slurped from his spoon, and his eyes were clouded and feverish as if his malaria had been aggravated by exposure.

During my nightwatch, the men wanted to know what happened to Paul. I knew only one would come back, Charles said. The sergeant said Paul wasn't gone yet, he's the toughest man here, and the doctor was smart, but not smart enough to get the better of Paul.

But he was poisoned with all that medicine, Charles said. The eldest arrival agreed with Charles that something was afoul with the doctor's return. Now the doctor's got the pregnant one all to himself, he said.

The sergeant said Paul had the best aim with a knife he'd ever seen. Could hit a squirrel on a tree ten yards away. Charles and the sergeant, the two men who had the most memories of Paul, began trading panegyrics about him, admitting he was too proud and certainly deranged, but it wasn't justified to take him away from the woman he loved.

They asked me how Sister M. was going to punish the doctor, but I told them no one had been accused of anything, and that Paul was probably back in the city, up to his ruffian antics again. My adamant reply further aggravated the men, perhaps because I did not trust in my own words, and the sergeant said that if the doctor could not be honest about what happened that night, then he had condemned himself.

Sister M. will file the disappearance with the parish officials, I told them. We can do nothing more.

You believe the doctor, what he said about the family taking him in, Charles asked. There aren't families living in the swamp, that's why they got us kept here, cause no one else's around. I think he did away with Paul and holed up in a hotel somewhere downriver. Can't trust a man who don't remember a thing.

The eldest arrival's coughing became violent until he sat up and rolled over to use his bedpan. After he was done, his breathing slowed down, each exhalation ending with a rattle in his throat, a sound that must have reminded Charles and the sergeant of Hans when he used to wheeze throughout the night.

Although I had slept but briefly after leaving the men's cabin, my eagerness to trace the river to Point Clair was undiminished. I moved through a darkness that relented with my steaming breath. Starlings and finches were riotous, cusped on that hour when first light would admonish them, bringing baffled repose to the canopy.

The levee's banks had crumbled with the last bout of rain and resembled battlements stoked by scavengers long after the siege. Past the jetty the folds of my habit sparked consort with the winds. The river lapped at the ruins and recoiled into its ashen chill. When the east glimmered, its course seemed to halt, freezing as it did in my dreams, the mud thinning out to a pale cast, retreating into vines and roots before being fully stunned into cessation.

There I imagined the two men standing. The doctor, with his diverse repository of lethal fluids, could have threatened to inject his patient, possibly forcing him into a trench that would swallow any evidence of his crime. Or perhaps it were Paul who held his knife to the doctor's back as their feet sunk into the earth, or pressed the blade to his throat while the doctor kneeled facing westward, away from the river's bend, clenching his hair to hold his neck taut, already having bound him in the scullery, and somehow the doctor grappled the knife away from Paul while they struggled, thrusting it into his patient's back as the morning winds shook them.

I scraped my boot in the grass, hoping to uncover some shred of clothing, or the weapon itself, but if there were some trace, the mud had buried it. Among the roots sprawling from the water, I found a fragment of a rudder, shoots of my beloved mallows, a turtle outstretched from its shell.

The two men would have come to that inlet only if Paul were the aggressor. I had never known the doctor to stray that far upriver when collecting lizards, but there seemed to be no mark of either man's presence, no discovery of malice to report to Sister M. or withhold in titillating secrecy. I incessantly overturned scenarios, imagined the two in their sacrificial poses with more vividness than any dream I could recall. My pulse quickened, and I hollered ruthlessly at the waters, not out of invective, but out of terror flaring through the nest of singed nerves in my brain.

Just as the patients were unperturbed by the doctor's absence, Sister M. did not seem worried by Paul's absence. What was one less patient to her but another empty cot, one less helpless soul to placate? She would file her report. The city health officials would add another name to their list of absconded pariahs, waiting to capture him while he begged before the cathedral, or visited his brother at the abattoir they owned together. If he were alive, they would find him, and if he were dead, then may the earth be purged of his disease.

I reenacted the moments of that night, but with each permutation, my memory became less believable, and, without a motive, the visions would become more sinister in effect, overpowering the mind that shaped them. Should I have accepted, like Sister M., that the total breadth of this mystery was that two men had disappeared and but one returned? Louise would not admit who impregnated her, and the doctor claimed only to remember falling asleep in his bed before he was found by a poacher miles from camp.

Though the patients may have believed a murderer tended their wounds, they had no choice but to submit to his care or otherwise waste away more rapidly. They would not miss Paul's bucolic asides, his aversion to bathing, his unwillingness to hand over his linens for washing, or his reproaches towards the staff because he was convinced he was being poisoned. If more patients were to arrive, he would have most certainly spread distemper among them, and his residence would have caused much more disunion than his disappearance.

I was back at the house shortly after sunrise. The kitchen

door was open, and the water had yet to boil. Both Sister E. and Sister M. prayed together in the dining room, conducting some séance to precede the long bustling that awaited them, not an altogether unusual practice in the morning, and one which I indulged in readily for it never became tiresome. After the dusty paneling and stench of humorless women peeled away, the great silence reigned. All I could do was subjugate my mind, wring my heartchords upon that fire everlasting, a pleasure more trying, and therefore more ecstatic than writing itself, which contained but half of prayer's equation, that is, I only listened to myself, and the source of unknowable splendor did not welcome my voice, only the cramped drawer of my desk did.

During those nights when I dozed in the men's cabin, listening to the patients defame the doctor, or lie about their prehistories, I had no time to sit at my desk and write myself to sleep. My hands were cramped, my memory depleted, but no corner was too profane for me to bow my head and follow my breath ever closer to the total renunciation of flesh, hoping to hear a voice whose words did not echo like mine own.

When the sheriff's men busted open the front doors of the house, the Mother, Sister M., and another sister who had left in the second year were led inside to tidy the floors and burn chair parts and rugs in the yard, preparing the house for two days before the first patients were brought by a tugboat named after a woman, as most boats are, which docked directly across the front gate and would be the last boat to do so.

The first patients encamped in the house before the cabins were made habitable, and I was certain, when the cabins became overcrowded, patients would reside in the house once again. If the holding terminal was emptying its cells, then we had to expect more arrivals after the next load, and all twenty-two rooms would be brimmed and besotted with phlegmatic choruses, faces made whole again by darkness, where we sidled past one another in and out of rooms, cued by groans and bells, canes slammed against the floor, shutters wrapped violently during our bedchamber hours, the commotion not quieting until one of us, most probably myself, arose to get dressed, light a candle, and creak down the hall.

When the patients resided in the house in those beginning months, the Mother and Sister M. had a third partner. I never asked them about her fate, this Sister whom I was later to replace, but the documents in the middle drawer of the parlor desk did not shield her inglorious exit: accusations of consorting with a soldier, starving patients into discipline before her reassignment to a hospital in a northern parish, but sometimes I wondered whether my fallen predecessor was a malingerer of sorts, playacting her madness to be rescued from the camp, sent to a veritable refuge, not a prison masquerading as one.

After recuperating in bed for two days, the doctor informed Sister M. that he would once again see patients in the scullery, but most of the patients did not trust him with whatever ailment they had, so he busied himself with drafting more experiments, tinkering in his medicine cabinet with unorthodox combinations that we assumed he was testing on himself to curb his fever.

I shared with Sister E. the task of bringing his meals after his two-day seclusion. Since the lizards dispersed, he began storing various serums in the bowls on his shelf. I did not see his beloved anole on those occasions when I carried the tray to his desk and inquired after his health, but I was confident that the lizard clung to a table leg or had buried itself in parchment whenever a stranger breached the doorway.

Charles and the enfeebled eldest arrival gossiped about Paul's disappearance as if it were already accepted camp lore. They had heard from the grandmother that the doctor confessed to Sister M. about what occurred the night of the celebration. He claimed Paul had knocked on his door after the bonfire had simmered, desperately beseeching the doctor to step outside. Once the two of them were in the yard, Paul attacked him with a hammer stolen from Charles.

There, the doctor's recounting of the night ended, and he didn't remember anything more until being awakened by the poacher miles away. Not an altogether implausible account, and the men were at a loss to dismiss it with any sound reasoning. Charles said that if Paul wanted to kill him, he would have done it in the scullery without hesitation, not dragged him into the yard where the last revelers slumbered in mud.

I did not see a bludgeoning mark on his head, nor was it true that the two men first struggled outside when the condition of the scullery attested otherwise. Was the doctor brazenly deceiving Sister M. and mocking her gullibility? The sergeant said the doctor did not need to confess because the wicked can easily forget what they have seen. Listening to their gossip, it seemed that the patients were privy to what occurred within the house before me, as if I were some chattelhouse mare too dullwitted to be trusted.

After I left the men to their fitful dreams, I waited on the backstoop until Sister E. came out of the women's cabin to ask her if the doctor had told her anything about Paul. She said that Sister M. had met with the doctor in the parlor after dinner. For Sister E., Paul had been consigned to the spirit of St. Anthony. His wayward soul did not belong with the restful, those on the path of self-abnegation.

When she spoke, I imagined her as a feral child tamed and coddled in turns by the rigorous ethic of her mistress, civilized by Thomist doctrine, transported from the pinewood darkness of Ontario to a place where civilization was pitilessly washed away, where doctrine could merely soothe the tongue which uttered it while the soul drowned repeatedly with each new rain, each levee breach, each roof collapse upon the near dead who rightfully mistrusted our care, yet nodded to accept it.

In the morning I led the Croat to the scullery for the beginning of his steam treatment. The Croat, typically softspoken, resisted my hand, slobbering his sibilant language. I assured him that the doctor was not going to hurt him, which was true insofar as the Croat was unaffected by physical pain due to his affliction, but the doctor's steaming of Este had not helped him to walk again however much sensation he regained in his legs. The Croat suffered boils on his thighs and infected pustules feasted on his toes, which we periodically scrubbed with a substance not unlike the one that poisoned Hans. Why's he working on him when Este still can't walk, the sergeant asked.

The doctor only knows how to make people worse, Charles said.

As we crossed the yard, the Croat wrenched his crutch from the mud with each step until he put his arm around my neck, holding the crutch in his other hand and dragging his injured leg. The scullery door was opened and the tank was already steaming. Before the Croat climbed inside, the doctor requested that I record more observations of the patient's legs. He measured abrasions on one leg and lesions on the other with his caliper while I entered his measurements in the patient's slim file. The doctor took the Croat's heart rate and tested his reflexes by tapping his knees with a mallet wrapped in rubber tubing and jabbing the bottom of his feet with his scalpel.

The Croat told the doctor the tank wasn't going to fix him, that he'd burned himself before, on his arms, and the hair never came back.

You didn't feel it burning you then, the doctor told him. You will not feel this either. The steam will burn all the toxins away, and your skin will heal itself. The bone will grow back, so you won't need that crutch anymore.

The doctor's tone was more earnest than before, less melancholic. It was as if his experience had refined itself, or as if his university learning had been dislodged and more readily accessible after he had been supposedly bludgeoned on the head. He convinced the Croat to enter the tank, and I helped him lift the patient from the table. The Croat clinched as he was submerged just as Este did, but when he felt little sensation from the heat, he stopped begging to be taken out of the tank, shutting his eyes while the steam enclosed his face.

I took up the pen, waiting for dictation, but the doctor said my assistance was not necessary while the patient was submerged. He would record any observations himself and call for me again once treatment was finished. After all, my labors were better applied to more onerous tasks because of my heft and penance.

I set the pen down and stood up from the desk, humiliated by his request, as if I could no longer be trusted with recording his words and observing a crippled man being dunked in a tank whose pleas were not heeded by another man, who paced nonchalantly beneath the plumes, a torturer in a white smock, but not extracting a confession like those torturers in black, unless any response to treatment is akin to revelation.

If the leg did not heal, then steam could not completely defeat the affliction, but this we knew already, and so did the doctor. Partly because I felt slighted by him, I voiced my doubt, asking him why he continued this treatment since Este's paralysis had not yet been cured.

Standing beside the open door, he said the patients must be willing to heal, but they are mistrustful of treatment. We have been careless, he told me. Much too generous with our concessions. Your Superior, Sister M., is right. Time not spent being vigilant encourages them to feel exempt from the camp's rule. They become stubborn, reckless. Each of them must be treated medicinally. Examinations must become routine. Why should the crudeness of one patient hinder the healing of others? If one patient seeks to destroy the camp, injure the staff's integrity, or another patient's honor, then that patient must either be curbed from his destruction or excised from the camp. The flock shall not fall for the lamb. Have we not discussed Leviticus before, Sister S?

He had not uttered my name in the past, and occasionally I wondered if he knew it at all, or if I would forever be known as the nameless nag, busied around by meek commands and priestly condescension. Stubbornly standing before the door, I asked him if he thought Paul would be captured and returned, and he said Paul was not fit for camplife, and now without him around the other patients could fully benefit from treatment.

Paul dishonored every patient, he said. Not just Louise. He interfered with their healing, and few crimes are worse.

He left me standing in the doorway and walked over to his desk while steam was rattling the lid. I looked across the yard and saw Sister E. climbing the steps of the women's cabin, carrying two buckets of water. All of the female patients were inside the cabin save for the new arrival who sat on the porch looking across the purdah trace where the mariner and Charles stood smoking, the tools used for repairing the walkway scattered in the yard.

The oaks were adorned with leaves coated thickly by wax. The river was empty of vessels as its tide shirked into a shade darker than earth for the clouds became bloated and bruised creatures, stagnant yet not ready to detonate. No wagons passed. The levee was a succession of parched, uneven mounds. More kitten litters appeared in the busted crawlspace behind the chapel. Vines spawned up the sides of the barn, and the cow would not budge for grazing, preferring starvation to the noon heat.

The scraps of distraction provided by the newest female arrival prevented the men from asking why the other women were barely ever seen outside their cabin. I told them I held no responsibility over the women's cabin, and the men were much too rowdy at night for me to hear Louise's cries. They caroused with their sex often exposed through their shredded drawers, boasting about how they would get revenge against the doctor, or betting on arm wrestling bouts, which rarely lasted more than a minute before the two combatants struggled on the floor, as if they were provoking me to interfere, reprimand them, and send them all off to bed. To the male patients, I had become the mistress of an orphanage whose veins where tinged with a cruelty unlike what they accused the doctor of exhibiting, in that it was not tied to a thirst for posterity carried over from city life, but rather was an unflagging adoration of wrathfulness and discipline, faith corrupted by Calvinist inbreeding.

One evening I saw the doctor leave the women's cabin, hatless, wearing spectacles, and carrying his satchel. His head was upturned, yet he did not look at me while I was crossing in the opposite direction toward the men's cabin with a tray of turnips I had picked from the garden lately left untended by the grandmother and the girl. They were caring for Louise whom I imagined clenching her linens in pain while her face was burrowed between the edge of her cot and the wall.

The doctor must have been telling her the infant would bear the affliction from its first breath and therefore would not be taken by the city health officials. How did he convince the rest of the women to allow him to inject her with the serum, if indeed he were trying to medicate the infant through its mother's veins? He once remarked to me how rare Louise's case was in the literature he had studied. Now he could either disprove or embolden the dominant theories about contagion, whether it was inherited or if proximity to the afflicted alone determined infection.

Ratherne led Cybele to their porch twice a day, in the early morning and during dusk. She could walk again on her own and would swipe at his arm if he tried to help her. She became less resistant when I offered to change her dressing and sat beneath the oak that shaded half the garden while her cabinmate smoked on the porch.

I dressed her with due tact and flourish, pinned all the frayed ends, and pulled the dressing taut so the shape of her cheekbones was not entirely concealed. Her breathing almost whistled through the fabric stuck to her septum, so I snipped sizeable holes around her nose and eyes. She said she wanted to feel sun on her face and see its light, since she thought she was going blind, but in truth her eyesight had not in the least diminished. From the garden she could still see Ratherne pacing the porch or a cat trailing the woodline. I bandaged her hands with similar care, accentuating her fingers, the elegant structure of which persisted through disfigurement, cutting or pinning the ends so that each finger could move easily even if her hands rarely left her lap.

Sister M. would stay in the parlor with the doors closed after dinner, allowing only Sister E. within to briefly discuss news regarding Louise, or give more expansive reports over the actions of other patients and myself. I was not permitted to enter the women's cabin, but Sister E. could visit the men's, where she blushed when Charles told her how the sight of her helped him feel better and that he had carved her name in one of the walkway slats.

If I ever saw Sister M., it was usually in the kitchen where she placed kindling in the oven, and her fingers would hover atop the coals until I retched at the scent of her burning flesh. The doctor commented on her wounds, offering to dress them, but she declined and insisted the injuries did not hinder her in the least. Her lack of appetite, increased fatigue, and sensitivity to light attested to more than malaria and yet she arose with each day, enshrouded herself, each cuff and fold and point neatly starched, and assigned me more tasks to do. She would not submit herself to the doctor's diagnostics, preferring to be ignorant of what consumed her, sitting alone in the closed parlor, turned away from the windows and relishing the house's quietness before patients took up the rooms once again.

Since both Mothers had become ill, I wondered if it were the position itself that had infected them. But contrary to what one might assume, Sister M. did not become more sympathetic to the patients through sharing the same infirmity. She pitied herself with beatific attrition. Just as she refused to acknowledge what invaded her flesh, she shied away from the evil that inhabited the camp.

One evening I spoke with her in the dining room about the male patients' distrust of the doctor. Her blistered hand was outstretched on the table while the tabby circled her legs. What good is having a resident physician, I asked her, if the patients reject his care. She answered that Louise is submitting to the doctor's care without obstinacy. It is the men who do not trust him, she said, and they are your responsibility.

I told her that I shared their mistrust, and the doctor implicated himself in Paul's disappearance. He lied about what occurred, I said, and he believes his crimes are justified.

Remember why you joined the Order, she said. You were abandoned by your father and by the man who took your hand. That is why I decided against you assisting the doctor. You have been reared to trust no man. Where were you orphaned again? The Mother let me read your file when you arrived. Ohio? Or was it further North? Somewhere in Canada?

I did not answer her. I thought she was confusing my past with Sister E.'s, or perhaps with the Sister who preceded me.

I am surprised, she said, that you listen to those spiteful men. They should be grateful for the doctor's tenure. No one else would dare replace him, and I fear we will not see a priest for another generation.

I left two trays of food on the porch of the women's cabin where the covered windows were brightly lit. Before I knocked, I listened at the door and heard voices muttering within. Since the scullery was dark, I guessed the doctor was inside the cabin as well, the basin set at the foot of the cot while Sister E. stood behind him with beads knotted in her grip.

I was in the garden uprooting turnips when I heard robust wailing from the women's cabin. The men were out on their porch, facing the furrow, and Ratherne and Cybele stood in the yard outside the third cabin, all of them listening to the infant announcing its exile from the womb.

Did you kill the kid's mother too, Charles asked the doctor, who was shuffling across the yard, his shirt and trousers bloodstained. The doctor said nothing as the men heckled him with the same words they used unrepentantly when I held nightwatch. The doctor's back was turned to me, but I heard the sergeant ask him what he was holding in a cup. The first woman to emerge from the cabin was Sister E. who brought me a bucket and asked if I would retrieve water. Both are alive, she said. But Louise's got the shivers.

The woman's cabin smelled of blood. The infant was sleeping in the grandmother's arms. I scrubbed the floorboards and peeled the sopping linens from the cot while Louise raved and seized and glared at me without recognition.

She still doesn't know what happened, said Sister E.

The grandmother wondered why she wouldn't look at her own child. He's more handsome than most, she said. And sprite at that.

Louise had turned from where the grandmother sat, trembling as Sister E. wiped her down with a rag. When the doctor entered the cabin again, he looked into the bucket where the placenta had spilled. He must have placed a sample of it in the tin cup earlier and was deciding whether to take more of it. The cabin was so quiet I could hear the infant breathing into his swaddles, the hem of the grandmother's dress rustling as she swayed, as if the women would not speak while the doctor was inside. After measuring the infant's temperature, he said he wanted to quarantine him in the house.

He should sleep next to his mother the first night, the grandmother said.

Keep the door open, he said, and leave the windows uncovered.

Before leaving the cabin, he asked me to bring the Croat to his office for another round of steam treatment. As I crossed the yard with the bucket, the men asked after Louise, and I told them she was faring better. The doctor did not seem as surprised by the survival of Louise and her child as I had expected him to be.

A month before he had spoken of a stillborn delivery as unavoidable, but he appeared neither relieved nor disappointed and hardly altered his schedule for the day. He must have known the arrival of more patients in the house would defeat any likelihood of successfully quarantining the child. No corner of the camp would exempt the infant from exposure to the affliction unless he were abandoned to the swamp and rescued by the same poacher who found the doctor, but such a fateful deliverance was too miraculous in our nation's dregs, where a miracle would sooner be washed away than witnessed by any living soul.

Heat had made the river more sullen. If mud from the bank did not dissolve, I would swear the tide was halted. I poured the bucket downriver from the front gate as its bloody slough plunged and vanished. Slowly the ripples unraveled and I could see the river's haggard flow. I waded further, both feet tickled by the depth currents, until the water crept to my stockings that were rolled up past my knees.

I was standing close to where I had found the Mother, guessing she was mad with fever when I called to her from the bank. When she stepped from the water, she was shivering and reached for her clothes while her hair dripped across her face. Perhaps she just fancied one final swim, and Sister M. was wrong to have locked her in her bedchamber all day and night after I led her back to the house.

I could see the worn tip of Point Clair from where I waded, and I imagined how slowly the tide would carry me if I lifted my legs, but then Sister E. would be left alone to cook, watch over the men, change Cybele's dressing, feed the cow, empty the bedpans, sweep the porches. If the Mother had heaped this many tasks upon my fallen predecessor, I would not be surprised if she authored her own exit purposefully by consorting with a patient.

According to our apostolic creed, the least experienced Sisters are apportioned with the most labor for their inexperience is tantamount to sinfulness, and the more onerous the task one fulfills, the more one's faith is demonstrated. However, if this practice were truly upheld, then Sister E. should have been given more physical labor. She arrived more than a year into my tenure and was assigned as a novitiate under my tutelage after which my tasks became more elevated, requiring less physical exertion. I assisted the priest, perfected my unruly bandaging, swept the porches occasionally and acted as Sister M.'s understudy in the kitchen, but her concoctions were often tasteless and soggy because she was too thrifty with coal.

My experience disserved me, however, because Sister M. was convinced I had sided with the male patients in their accusations against the doctor, but I agreed with her that the male patients were bitter vagrants, apt to resent anyone who told them when to eat and sleep. She was right to say that I had lost trust in men, especially those who waggled their authority unremittingly, and who bedecked their shelves with polished instruments and specimens of worldly conquest. But no matter her accusations, I trusted in my vision of that murderous night. A man's body with a decisive knife wound across his neck who tumbled down the levee, trailed by a ribbon of blood as he floated downriver. It was the Metairie butcher, the roustabout, the ravisher of Louise whose violent end we were probably right not to mourn.

The infant was brought inside the house. Because it was difficult to coax him from the grandmother's arms, we permitted her and the girl entrance into the house to care for him during the afternoons. No one gave him a name, but his vigorous kicking and bellicosity reminded the female patients of Paul. In the cleanest upstairs room, we set a washed cot atop the bedframe and lifted the shutters, draping them in netting. I struggled to milk the cow because of its hardened utter, but I was able to retrieve enough so that the grandmother could nurse him each morning.

Before he had barely repaired a foot's length of the walkway, Charles set to work building a crib. Some of the men gathered around Sister E. in the yard while she held the infant. The sergeant also claimed he reminded him of Paul. He's got that little puckered mouth, he said.

Their vengefulness against the doctor was lessened by their excitement over the birth, as if it had brought tidings of health and exuberance. The only patient seemingly disappointed by his birth was Louise who, according to Sister E., tried to kill him the first night he slept by her side, but the infant erupted in squeals as

Louise was not strong enough to smother him with her pillow. The other women awoke, and the girl shone a lantern on the infant who writhed beside Louise with a flushed face.

Sister E. agreed with me that quarantining the child was useless if the patients were permitted inside the house as well. The longer he remains here, I told her, the more endangered he will become. The doctor wishes to experiment on him. To see if he will become afflicted. He has already taken a piece of the placenta to examine.

She claimed the doctor had been tender in his treatment towards both Louise and the infant and did not share my distrust. He has protected him against his own mother, she said. From the beginning, she begged the doctor to drown out her womb and has never spoken of that child as her own. And when the other women scolded her for what she had done, he alone took up her honor.

I wondered why the doctor was suddenly so eager to uphold a patient's honor when he had once told me they were akin to the criminally insane. Perhaps Sister M.'s fixation with honor had lately influenced him, but surely they both knew honor would not feed and cloak and purify them.

The postboy was the first passerby I had seen trailing the levee since that beleaguered pair with the carriage weeks before the celebration. I recognized him from the previous delivery for his bulky satchel hindered his long gait, and I recalled his fearful stare, his unease at completing the last stop of his route.

He hurriedly unloaded a rectangular parcel and two envelopes, retreating closer to the levee as I reached to grab them. The parcel was addressed to the doctor, presumably one of the new instruments he had ordered. One envelope was addressed to Sister M. from the holding terminal while the other was addressed to the Irish surname of the eldest arrival, presumably a reply from his estranged spouse.

Before the boy could tip his hat, I asked him if he attended church in town. He said he was Methodist.

And does your pastor speak of this place, I asked.

He nodded.

And what does he say?

He says nothing there can hurt you lest you think on it, the boy said. I smiled and told him he did right to listen to his pastor, but his eyes avoided both the house and his interlocutor. After he tipped his cap and turned around, I prayed that he would continue to run his routes and be familiar with every citizen within ten square miles of his town, eventually commandeering the post office, marrying a local girl, engendering a sturdy flock, and afforded a dignified peace in his final years. Or perhaps the river would tempt him onward, a stowaway to the city, far from the decrepit town which would soon be known only for its closeness to the camp, after our borders expanded to accommodate the incoming hordes and overlapped with the surrounding canefields, overtaking the town's streets and alleys, till the unspoken and the everyday merged into one pestilent swamp.

Because of her frailty in the heat, Sister M. did not meet me on the porch to collect the post, but she was watching from the parlor window. Some rituals of the camp never changed. Before I handed the parcel and envelopes to her, she had already donned her spectacles. She closed the parlor doors with more weariness than the day before, when I saw her gripping the banister and offered my arm to support her, but she said I would be more useful in the kitchen and strained harder to climb the steps. I expected her to retire again in the early evening, and I busied myself with remonstrating Lucas for not bathing, and prepared supper.

After returning to the kitchen with the patients' bowls and utensils, I heard Sister M. and Sister E. conversing in the dining room. Sister M. softened her voice when she heard me in the kitchen, but Sister E. lent stridency to her otherwise meek demeanor and said that she could not trust her mission here if the child were endangered.

I entered the dining room to remove their plates and saw both letters on the table. Sister M. propped herself up by the table's edge, her cornice pushed tight against her pale face. She grabbed both letters and requested that Sister E. follow her to the parlor.

That night my invocation over the washbasin was reduced to a few lackluster prayers, the vision of a woman birthing a towheaded infant in a pious house on a sunken shore, the midwife presenting the infant to a husband who stood in the corner with hat in hand, gloating over its resemblance to himself. The woman was aware after her torment subsided that she would do better to stay on her back as he would soon require her loving submission after the infant was christened.

Sister E. returned to the infant's room, and our Superior retired to her chamber after barely a spoonful of broth. Inside her desk, I found the two letters neatly folded beneath an ink jar. Both were from the holding terminal. One was announcing a new shipment of patients in the following month, perhaps the hottest month of the year, the other confirmed that dry goods would be delivered at the end of the current month. At least they were courteous enough to send separate shipments. The patients would not fare well by ingesting goods contaminated by their own malady.

The letter was addressed 'Dear Honorable Sisters' and ended with an illegible signature. There it was once more: the same appeal to honor which the doctor had resorted to when speaking of the patients' dignity. He was echoing the false reverence of the officials who had employed him. According to this unknown signee, the increase in patients was not the preference of the holding terminal, especially since they were well aware of how understaffed the camp was, but the city government had a constituency to placate, commerce to conduct, and such a large population of afflicted persons within its limits was untenable. A proposition had been voted on by the State and thus an exodus upriver would begin. All of this was of course stipulated in their pervious letter, but now they were informing us that emptying the holding terminal was legally upheld, perhaps because in her last letter Sister M. had requested proof of higher authorization.

The next expected shipment of dry goods would be doubled to suit the recently added patients and those to come. Carpentry supplies, cots, kerosene, and bandages would also be delivered. The first portion of the letter must have terrified Sister M., whereas the concluding paragraphs worked to conciliate her by dulling the specter of invasion.

She had become what she had tirelessly sought to distinguish herself from, a helpless subjugate to her own flesh. She could no longer attend to the affliction in others, for it had now befallen her. Luckily, the camp would partly shield her from the outer world's ostracism. If she were to be infected anywhere, what better place than at camp, where her malady was mundane, where she had a spacious upstairs dwelling, a slovenly throne in which to convalesce.

I refolded the letters and placed the ink jar atop them. Then, I closed the double doors and mopped the kitchen. If I had decided to go upstairs to discuss the letter with Sister E., I risked awaking Sister M., so I waited till she came downstairs after coaxing the child to sleep.

We spoke on the back porch where she agreed that the infant could not be kept safe if he resided here, and that to punish him with the affliction was unforgivable. She told me she saw bruises on his arm when she went up to excuse the women from his room. They confessed the doctor had drawn blood from him, she said.

I reminded her about the barge arriving soon with supplies. If it's just the pilot, I said, he could be easily swayed with payment.

And if an official rides with him?

We would have a note from Sister M. approving of the decision.

But she would never allow it.

I told her that our Mother would soon be too feeble to

be concerned either way, and if one of us were to ride with the child, we could leave him at the city's cathedral. There the bishop's adjutant would secure him an orphanage. I did not tell her how I had mastered Sister M.'s signature long ago to amuse myself when bedchamber hours were ample, when I also would imitate Sister M.'s gestures and locution in a rather unflattering manner.

Although she agreed that we must take the child away, she was too anxious at that moment to commit to doing it. I also did not want to leave the camp, but not because I was worried of disobeying Sister M. or the Order. The prospect of disembarking onto the city's docks was far more harrowing than knowing my fate was confined to the camp.

I told her we had to betray Sister M. if we wanted to rescue the child, and if we left him at the doorstep of the church in the closest town, someone there may suspect where he was from and bring him back here. I considered leaving him at the poacher's cabin, but that was also unfavorable compared to taking the infant to the city, since my knowledge of the terrain beyond the camp's borders was altogether deficient. I could have circled a shack for days before chancing upon it, which would certainly endanger the child more than a two nights floating downriver, and if the doctor's story were honest, the poacher and his family would have been exposed to the affliction when sheltering him during his recuperation.

Whenever the doctor visited the child, Sister E. made certain she was also in the room. Sister M. did not leave her bed until late morning, and the doctor, who had inquired about her health, was led to her room where he determined she had contracted the affliction. The numbness in her toes was the decisive sign, and, according to Sister E., our Superior received his diagnosis begrudgingly, but agreed to undergo treatment. The doctor advised Sister M. not to go outside in case sunlight worsened her condition, advice which most of the patients declined to follow, risking bouts of blindness and ulcerous outcroppings on their arms and necks.

I did the washing early and hung clothes at the north wing. Through the tattered trousers and nightshirts, I watched where the barges docked upriver. A gust held the sopping linens at an oblique angle from the ground. Sweat had so encased me I could not feel the wind brushing by, or else I had become infected like Sister M. and was therefore numb to its touch. During that part of the year, all we could expect was the cypresses to melt, the cats to remain ravenous, and heat to bury our stale fantasies with a dirge sung by the scratching breeze.

I went to the rear of the house and put the basket inside the kitchen. Before I was set to prepare lunch, I went to the men's cabin to see if any bandaging needed to be done, then retrieved the Croat for more steam treatment. The scullery door was open and the tank was already boiling. The doctor told me to return in an hour's time and said he would take his lunch then.

From his porch, Ratherne was watching the sky where a plume of smoke was trailing. Charles and the mariner were on the porch of the men's cabin, enthralled by the female arrival pacing before them in a frail smock with her face shaded by a bonnet.

I hurried around the northwing to the road so I could greet the barge before the hospital emissary came to our gate. The walkway had already been set across the water, and the emissary had carried a few crates across it.

We need to transport one of our sisters downriver, I said. She has urgent matters in the city.

The emissary was too distracted by a missing receipt to rightly address my request. He said he heard nothing of it from his superiors, and that it was the pilot's boat anyways. I crossed the deck to the stern where the pilot had dropped a string into the water. I was sure to stay a few feet away so the infected folds of my dress did not alarm him.

Another body won't sink us, he said. I can take her down. I told him we would pay the fare like any passenger. Just tell her to bring her luck with her, he said. Behind us the emissary called out that he had found the receipt, and I told him I would get the Mother to sign it. Then, we loaded two barrels and a crate of cutlery atop a handwagon, which we pulled down the road to the front gate.

Lucas was standing in the yard and asked if he could ride the wagon, but I told him to go see Louise as the emissary seemed unsettled by the boy's presence. With receipt in hand, I climbed the stairs and stepped lightly down the hall to the room where Sister E. was humming a lullaby as the infant dribbled milk down its chin. She turned and saw the receipt and asked if it was time to go, holding the infant tightly to her breast.

I told her they would take her downriver, and she peered through the shutters. Wait up here, I said, going quietly downstairs into the parlor where I dipped the pen and mimicked our Superior's signature on the receipt and slipped it in my vestment pocket. The emissary was waiting where I left him, turned toward the river as if looking at the house too long were tantamount to waltzing with a patient.

We repeated our run from the barge to the house another four times and on the last trip he asked me how come I had no help from the other Sisters. I told him I was stout in flesh, but feeble in spirit.

It's like me and Schultz, the pilot, he said. He doesn't ever bother with the cargo.

If you tell him to wait, will he listen?

Schultz's gonna leave after he gets a catch, the emissary said.

Before some wily catfish was wrenched from the waters, I had an array of preparations to make, questions to avert, ploys to fabricate. I left Sister E. to invoke St. Christopher with his callused feet and polished staff, a man who never seemed to stay in one place long enough to be a reliable figure for prayer.

The Croat was getting dressed when the doctor opened the scullery door. Before I left, holding the Croat's hand, I told the doctor that Louise had not taken to her medicine, a guiltless ruse that would give Sister E. and myself a good half hour before he thought about inquiring after the deliveries, or visiting the infant upstairs. Some of the male patients were on the porch, offering to bring supplies inside the kitchen, but I did not trust their eagerness to help, which was rather eagerness to horde food in their pockets or see what they could steal later when the downstairs was unguarded.

The emissary had by then probably returned to the barge where the pilot was wiping down the deck, his line still cast in the water, undisturbed by the depths. At last I was gracious for the opaque river where the fish were blinded, their fins caught in the viscous fold.

I brewed a small portion of hibiscus tea with periwinkle as sedative for the infant. From the bottom of the stairwell, I heard his wailing and carried the basket up to the landing and saw that Sister M.'s bedchamber was still sealed.

Before the shuttered window, Sister E. was swaying with the infant whose head rested on her breast. He finally suckled the tea after I mixed it with cow's milk. She did not want to lower him inside the basket, but I told her they were waiting for us and led her from the window.

What if he cries for milk?

By then they won't want to turn back, I said. We heard Sister M.'s coarse cry down the hall, calling out for Sister E., who renounced her hold and let me put him inside the basket. I can't leave him in the city, she said. An orphanage is no better than here.

Let shame be stricken from my testament. Virtue belongs to the courageous, not to those who have renounced their dignity. Although Sister M. did not know we had the infant with us, she suspected some mutinous cunning, which she had hitherto associated with the patients.

She followed us down the hall, slowed by her stiff legs, yelling at us to stop from the top of the stairs. When she saw me opening the door, she slipped on the first step, grasping onto the stairwell as her left leg bent beneath her. Sister E. hurried to the front porch with the basket. I pulled a parasol from the coat rack before closing the door while our Superior sat on the top of the stairs, clenching her leg and threatening me with expulsion from the Order, even though she must have known her authority was purely nominal for she had joined the ranks of the afflicted.

In the front yard the sergeant and the mariner had already opened some barrels, and the latter had molasses smeared on his chin.

Sister E. hurried down the road, following the smoke traces. She had no change of clothes, no assurance of a return trip, no knowledge of the city's streets, but she stepped onto the barge steadfastly, declining the emissary's offer to carry the basket for her while she crossed the walkway.

The pilot had reeled his line and lifted anchor and was already in his cabin, prone above the wheel. Sister E. sat at the bow with the parasol spread out to shade both her and the basket held between her knees. Because I feared the sight of the barge drifting away would rouse my regret, I turned and trudged up the levee without waving goodbye.

Sister M. was still on the stairs, and I led her to the parlor divan where she remained until I had installed one of the cots we received in a downstairs room. Through the kitchen window, I saw Charles on the men's porch, passing out cigarette cartons to the mariner and the sergeant from a recently delivered crate.

I was confident Sister M.'s reliance on me would slowly temper her accusations and insults, but I was wary of ever usurping her position. Whoever occupied it seemed to be met by malediction.

The doctor would likewise quell his outrage at losing a valuable subject for his experiments. He may have wished to imprison me in the barn, or lure me into the swamp and abandon my defrocked body to the mud's embrace, but he relied on my labor just as Sister M. did, and, when he asked me why I had allowed Sister E. to steal away with the infant, I answered she was undeterred by my pleas to remain at camp. She had convinced herself that she was the child's savior, I told him, and even the Mother could not thwart her intentions.

He visited Sister M. in the downstairs room to set her broken leg and continue his serum treatment to seize the progress of the disease. The two of them probably conferred and decided I could not be trusted with managing the camp alone, and Sister M. may have tried to convince the doctor that I was just as blameworthy for the infant's escape as Sister E. was, but until a priest arrived to settle the dispute and punish me for my insubordination, I would continue making my rounds while shouldering the house's upkeep.

Charles was also troubled by Sister E.'s flight. So much of his willingness to work was due to her coy encouragement, but I told him she would soon be among us again, however much I doubted she would return after the city enveloped her with its temptations.

The grandmother and the girl were saddened by the infant's departure, but they agreed with the other patients that he was better off somewhere else. As far as they knew, the affliction had not befallen him, and they were more relieved than mournful of the loss.

I was standing over the washbasin when I began to fashion images of youth, partly to divert myself from the sting of the soap on my chaffed knuckles and partly to discover whether by imagining a childhood I could distill legitimate memories, bemoaning throughout my entire invocation my lack of pen or parchment, and as I conjure these memories now, I cannot resist but to limewash the fresco and begin once more with a man whom I remember to be my father, a woman who reminds me of my mother, and a scattering of births during the prolonged thaw in the back bedroom where the woman screams so that heaven may attend, and the man drunkenly paces the hallway, this same man whom I will designate as father and who would lead me through the alleys where boys burnt toads and men unloaded barley carriages, and he would not speak for a year after his wife or the woman whom I may designate as mother died during the birth of the fifth child, and the alley ran alongside the gray lake's edge where bells rung continuously as barges docked in the city that could be considered my place of birth, but more than that, my hometown, where men would stray from their vessels through alleys in a cacophonous swarm of languages, but the father would not speak to them nor to his five children, and the eldest embarked with the sailors while the rest were taken by a young woman whom I could designate as the sister of the dead mother to the rectory of a church across the lake in a neighborhood of the city she had hitherto avoided, and this church would feed the children and teach them how to read and write and some of the siblings would ran away, and the youngest would die while those who remained learned the rudiments of classical tongues and astronomy and drafting, and on the tenth anniversary of the mother's death a fire would sweep through the city and spread to the church, leaving the sisters and the children to

157

disperse and the rows of clapboards where I may claim to have been born to become dissolute enclaves, and the house where the mother died birthing the fifth child was nearly unrecognizable with its collapsed roof and host of beleaguered denizens seen carousing through the windows and the view of the lake from the alley was disrupted by the construction of a hotel where sailors and dockworkers would later partake in ignominy, and those who lived on that street during the recollected childhood have no knowledge of the father's whereabouts, claiming that the sister of the dead mother absconded with a salesman and the house soon became empty, and, when the fire descended upon the neighborhood, the house where I may claim my childhood occurred was one of the few houses spared, but these memories belatedly recorded after the initial invocation over the washbasin seem confined to familial concerns, or decisive episodes of my education, rarely do sensory traces manifest themselves through recollection save for perhaps the gunmetal sheen of the father's beard, or the scent of paraffin which occasionally dripped from the hallway lantern, otherwise the frieze I have wrought appears rather dull, a litany of declarative statements which, when arranged chronologically, resemble any housewife's obituary, albeit missing the final panels rendered as an exodus to the frontier with the enterprising bridegroom who inherited his great uncle's claim and the felling of the forest until the once abundant claim becomes scorched by drought and the frontier wife in the final panel scavenges the fields for fruit and worms while her husband dies of erysipelas, his countenance too frightful for the children's eyes, and as the fires of a straggling tribe glow from the mountain pass she vows to let no one ever die in her arms again, and yet even my apocalyptic coda appears counterfeit and uninspired, another life culled from dimestore novelettes, resembling a million other lives, if none at all, and since the final panel presents a woman fending off hunger, I must leave the remainder of her fate unimagined as I attempted to fashion the experiences of youth, and the woman whom I may designate as myself would seem to already have eclipsed my own age, or at least what the registry in the parlor drawer determines my age to be, and I have never birthed children as the wideness of my hips prove deceptive, but my body nevertheless has been sequestered by a man, and yet any remnant of sensation has evaporated, forcing me once more to rely on the tales of seduction and infamy spun in tobacco shop romances, portraying this imagined self as the foolish maidservant who visits the barn after her chores are completed, and the master and his family have retired, to tussle with the stablehand in the loft while a grizzled piebald shuffles beneath them, those cold nights clasped together, their damp bodies itching beneath the wool as steam lifted from the piebald's snout, and the stablehand told her of his inherited claim three nights westward by train and two nights by carriage, beseeching her to be his wife and to settle the land alongside him, and yet the prospect of leaving the city of her youth frightens her, and what is more, she will lose the chance of seeing her father wandering the clapboard alleys, decrepit and shoeless, searching in turn for the house where his first wife died birthing his fifth child, and yet in his stupor he is unable to recognize the house repainted with its fallen roof and paper lanterns and lace curtains and bottles strewn in the yard, the same alleys she chances upon on her Sunday leave, but then she had years ago accepted the unlikelihood of ever seeing him again, and she still was undecided on what she would actually do if ever confronted with her father and she deferred the stablehand's fierce proposals until the mistress discovered the affair when she went to her chamber one evening and found it empty, sending the butler, a stout Pole who more than once pressed her up against the volumes in the master's library, to search the grounds for her whereabouts, quickly suspecting the barn for what he lacked in charm, he compensated with keen awareness, and the master that night banished the furtive lovers from the house in a ceremonial rite of shaming, whereupon the Polish butler hurled her meager belongings in the street, and the master horsewhipped the stablehand for trespassing and insulting the honor of his house while the mistress cursed her with the worst words one woman may use

159

against another, words which stirred the neighborhood with their shrill timbre, and after she gathered her belongings into the valise she had brought with her some eighteen months hence, the two lovers dashed down the street, the stablehand holding his soiled cap upon his head as they ran, smiling at her with his bloody lip, and her knowledge of the alleys led them to the main station where they huddled on the platform throughout the night, waiting for the eight-fifteen to Tulsa, and he would startle each time the stationmaster sounded his whistle, recalling the Pole who whistled for the police as they ran down the street, and he watched the illuminated clock hanging from the rafter, and when the train crossed the borders of the city she may designate as her hometown, he asked where she wished to be married, and she envisioned a stark ceremony on the prairie, conducted by a pastor on a horse, her veil thrashed by dust and after the vows were made, both the pastor and the groom fire their pistols in the air and the storm lifts the earth as the pastor rides away, firing his pistol and the bride and groom shelter in a barn, consecrating their nuptials and enacting reverence for their inaugural night together in the master's stable, and as she envisioned her savage wedding, the stablehand wondered whether marriage suited the character of their new domain, and if perhaps they should scorn the conventions of the past if they truly sought to tame these desolate lands, for their devotion, he claimed, would not be redeemed by ceremony, but would be forged through toil and cultivation, and the laws of Christ do not preempt these desolate lands, they must be set forth and thereafter defended and upheld against the bloodlust of other men.

Nearly a month had passed since Sister E. escaped with the infant, and I still wondered whether she was waiting to board an upriver barge to return to camp, or if she refused to part with the infant and boarded a riverboat destined for some northern city.

If it had been me who disembarked on the city's wharves, I could never have imagined returning to the camp. Perhaps I might have found another hospital to employ me, or relocated to some convent where the affliction was all but an archaic trope. At either a hospital or a convent, daily life was regimented enough to not be entirely dissimilar from the rituals I forged at camp, but returning to the outer world may have allowed more memories from my previous life to resurface. The ones who had left me, and the ones I had let die. The delinquent father with his poisoned gullet, the recalcitrant husband who thought he obtained an orphan bride, not a brooding mystic whose faith consumed his own. I could have returned to other rivers that broke and bent and fed into shimmering lakes shaded by slopes of timber. If the blessing of the city was in its anonymity, then the camp blessed me with forgetfulness, the final promise of absolution.

I spent the days unpacking supplies and dusting empty rooms, preparing the house for the next delivery of patients. I nailed the door to Sister M.'s bedroom shut for the air within it had always reeked of cat hair and sour flesh, and the bed was much too decadent for my liking. When the new patients arrived and overtook the house, I decided to let them fight over who deserved that regal room and its feathery throne.

When I brought biscuit and eggs to Sister M. each morning in the downstairs bedroom, she asked if a letter from the archbishop regarding the priest assignment had arrived yet. She still wanted to sit at her desk to balance accounts and draft letters, but her leg was too damaged for her to move about. Each time the doctor visited her, he administered one injection of serum and one of morphine, after which she was left to her prolonged stupor. The less aware she was of what occurred in camp, the more restful she would be.

I continued to perfect my bandaging, empty bedpans, wash linens, and scrub cots once a week with lime. On the Sabbath, Lucas rang the bell in the yard while I unlatched the chapel doors and swept the floor. The Croat usually sat alone on the front bench and stared intently at my hands during service while the boy lingered in the aisle until Communion, after which he ran outside, leaving the doors open for Ratherne and Cybele to enter and kneel at the altar.

The offer of wine was not enough to lure the other patients to the chapel, but my care had never been given as recompense for their faith. It was rather the consequence of my own inequity before divine judgment. The grandmother shared some of my cooking duties, and when I saw that rice or meal had been taken from the kitchen, I did not pursue the culprit. Rather, I designated all food from the house for common use. The patients nonetheless complained of hunger while I let the fat on my bones sustain me. After supper was eaten, I hunched over the washbasin as cats paced the dooryard, foolishly hoping for scraps. The men had begun to distill spirits and in the evenings they sometimes careened on the porch and scuffled while the female arrival laughed from within.

Because the stillness that presided within the house would soon wither, I cherished its brevity and sat in the parlor divan after Sister M. was put to bed. I tied the curtains back and opened the shutters. The gleam from the candlelight shook across the broken clock, the chairs with their shredded upholsteries, and the books lining the shelves. Sister M.'s tabby roamed the hallway and sometimes scratched at the parlor door. When I let it inside, it slinked against my legs before curling beneath the desk to fall asleep. Each night I removed a different book from the shelf. In winter they would probably be tossed into the fireplace by those patients unwilling to venture outdoors for kindling.

I awoke from the divan with a cramped back each morning, a book lying facedown on the rug. Thrushes were always the first to sound, long before shapes of branches could be parsed from the sky.

I kneeled before the window till dawn, when the visions from my prayers had not yet faded, and the river appeared to thaw. Mist lifted from the wet grass. The canopy drooped slowly to slake its thirst from the night wind. Borne of an unforgiving cataclysm, mud combed through the yard, rose up the porchsteps, and cracked through the glass before it coldly seeped around my knees.

NEW PLAINS PRESS
AUBURN, ALABAMA

www.ingramcontent.com/pod-product-compliance
Lightning Source LLC
Chambersburg PA
CBHW060244030726
47493CB00025B/2255